Tales from the

Henry Holt and Company   New York

Homeplace

Adventures of a Texas Farm Girl

Harriet Burandt and Shelley Dale

To Irene Hutto Krumrey,

who shared her memories and has given her

support so lavishly to all those she loves. Without

her, none of this would have been possible.

Thanks, Mom, from both Shelley and me.

—H. B.

For my parents, June and Norman Albin,

and my children, Sascha and Arlo.

—S. D.

Henry Holt and Company, Inc.
Publishers since 1866
115 West 18th Street
New York, New York 10011

Henry Holt is a registered trademark of
Henry Holt and Company, Inc.

Published in Canada by Fitzhenry and Whiteside Ltd.,
195 Allstate Parkway, Markham, Ontario L3R 4T8.

Library of Congress Cataloging-in-Publication Data
Burandt, Harriet.
Tales from the homeplace: adventures of a
Texas farm girl/
by Harriet Burandt and Shelley Dale.
p.   cm.
Summary: Nine stories capture the life of twelve-year-old
Irene Hutto growing up on a cotton farm in Texas in the 1930s, based
on the life of Harriet Burandt's mother.
[1. Family life—Texas—Fiction.   2. Farm life—Texas—Fiction.
3. Texas—Fiction.]   I. Dale, Shelley.   II. Title.
PZ7. B9154Tal   1997 [Fic]—dc20   96-38191

ISBN 0-8050-5075-2
First Edition—1997
Designed by Meredith Baldwin

Printed in the United States of America on acid-free paper.∞
1 3 5 7 9 10 8 6 4 2

Contents

Irene's Family Tree

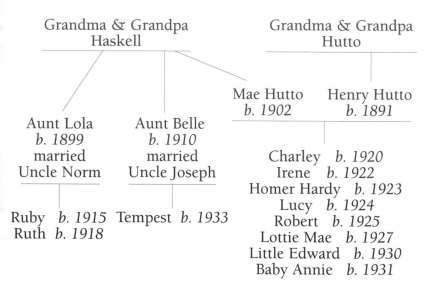

Grandma & Grandpa
Haskell

Grandma & Grandpa
Hutto

Mae Hutto
b. 1902

Henry Hutto
b. 1891

Aunt Lola
b. 1899
married
Uncle Norm

Aunt Belle
b. 1910
married
Uncle Joseph

Charley   *b. 1920*
Irene   *b. 1922*
Homer Hardy   *b. 1923*
Lucy   *b. 1924*
Robert   *b. 1925*
Lottie Mae   *b. 1927*
Little Edward   *b. 1930*
Baby Annie   *b. 1931*

Ruby   *b. 1915*   Tempest   *b. 1933*
Ruth   *b. 1918*

Tales from the Homeplace

The Panther

"Mae, come on!" called Daddy from the truck.

"I'm coming, Henry. Y'all be sure to watch for copperheads down by the creek," Mama called over her shoulder as she went down the porch steps.

Mama and Daddy were barely out the door and on their way to Robstown when Homer started in.

"C'mon, Irene, let's go to the creek. It's hotter than Hades today."

"Mama warned you, Homer Hardy. Stop jumping up and down in front of my face! I bet your freckles bounce right off your face one day. And you stop copying Homer, Robert. You heard Mama: no mischief, or when they get back there'll be some red backsides! Lucy, you get Baby Annie's bonnet and yours and then we'll walk on down to the creek. If anyone gives me any smart talk or starts fooling around, you're coming straight back here. Y'all understand?"

"Yes, MA'AM!" declared the children in one loud burst.

"And when I say it's time to get out of the creek, I mean get out. None of your ducking and splashing and staying under till I think you've drowned." Irene jammed her hands onto her hips like Mama, putting on a stern expression. "Did you hear me, Homer Hardy? Robert? Well?"

Both boys stuck out their lean chests and clamped their hands on their hips belligerently, mimicking their sister.

"Yes'm, yes'm. You don't have to act so bossy just 'cause you're in charge."

Irene raised her shoulders and tried to use her advantage of being a few inches taller than her brothers. She resisted the urge to smack their elbows. "I didn't ask to be the oldest girl. And now I can't even go swimming myself. I'm not going to put up with any of your back talk. So don't you be trying it today. Soon as I get some milk and biscuits for the baby we can go. And stop 'ma'aming' me as if I'm a teacher."

Irene reached up to the hook for her mother's apron, and then filled one large pocket with biscuits, and one with the baby's milk bottle. She pulled the apron over her head, tied it carefully around her waist, and fixed her sunbonnet under her chin, checking to see if Lucy and Lottie Mae had theirs tied as well. Wrapping Baby Annie in her shawl, she counted five heads and opened the screen door. She glanced toward the shotgun in the wall rack and thought, I certainly can't carry a baby and a loaded shotgun and watch five children with one pair of hands. Besides, she didn't think she'd have the nerve to shoot.

I don't know what Mama and Daddy expect, she thought as she let the door slam behind her. I'm still growing up here myself, how'm I supposed to figure everything out? Lucy's almost as old as me. It wouldn't hurt for her to practice being in charge once in a while, instead of acting so dreamy all the time about being a writer in Paris when she grows up. I wish Charley had been a girl. What good is it to have an older brother when I'm still the one who does all the baby-sitting? I bet Grandpa stops at the general store and buys him a soda at the store, too. "Darn," she cussed out loud.

Following the children down to the creek, Irene felt as if her bare feet were frying on the dirt road. Dust blew into her face as the others raced one another along the rows of cotton and sorghum. She blew the gnats off the baby's face. Even they were moving slower than usual in the heat.

"Baby Annie," she sighed, shifting the youngster to her other hip, "you're getting awfully heavy. I'm never going to make my daughter miss swimming just because she's the oldest." No one can carry me anymore, Irene realized. I guess Daddy or my grandpas could if they had to, like in Lucy's books. Irene leaned her head against Annie's sweaty blond curls and pictured herself being carried by one of the handsome Frenchmen Lucy was always writing stories about. Baby Annie pulled her head away, crinkling up her blue eyes and giggling. She drooled onto Irene's shoulder, then touched Irene's freckles one by one with her gooey finger, playing their counting game. Fixing Irene with a smile, the baby gave another giggle, ran her finger down Irene's slender nose and right up into her nostril.

"Eene!" squeaked Annie as Irene grabbed her chubby little finger and held it.

"Yep, that's me," she said. "I know it's not your fault I have to baby-sit, but stick your finger up your own nose, thank you."

"Hey, Irene," yelled little Edward in his husky voice. "Hurry! We're going in!"

Irene could see a pile of clothes on the bank as she rounded the last bend. She spread out the shawl close to the bank and gave a habitual search for snakes by stomping loudly around and peeking in the surrounding thorn bushes before she sat down with Annie propped between her legs. At least if it were spring, the creek would be high enough to cool my feet, she thought. Leaning over, she peered into the water for garfish. Irene could never believe that such large ugly fish could be in such a small creek, even if they were harmless. They were longer than she was tall, and had teeth that looked like Mama's pinking shears. Irene hoped Edward didn't spot one today and start his fearful screaming. It was just too hot for fussing.

"Don't you dare splash Annie and me, Homer, or you're going to make everyone get out." Irene would have liked the cool water, but if she let her brothers get started, they'd never mind her. She looked across the creek toward the wasatch and mesquite trees, absentmindedly reaching for a few strands of hair to chew on. Darn, she thought, as she remembered Mama's new haircut was to keep her from chewing and to make her look neater. She settled for twirling a strand with her finger. Irene could see the tracks of animals in the dried mud along the banks where they'd come to drink during the night. The creek was the only source of water for miles. If Corpus Christi Bay is so big, I don't know why they can't send some of it here, she wondered. She thought maybe it had something to do with the bay being salt water. Our well is salty, but we have to drink it. Maybe the fish and animals could get used to it, too. Then we'd have enough for everybody all summer. She'd have to remember to ask Daddy or Grandpa about this.

Irene felt the sweat trickle down her back and wished she'd left her underslip off today. But at least a dress was cooler than overalls. She had to be careful not to let the hot sun make her doze off. Even the armadillos seemed to be napping. Usually she saw at least one poking along on her way to the creek.

A bird shrieked overhead, and Irene glanced toward a movement on the opposite bank, hoping to see a jackrabbit pop up.

"Oh my Lordy," she said softly. Staring straight at her and Baby Annie from behind a bush was a panther. A large tan paw was barely visible behind the bare roots. Suddenly she understood why some people called them mountain lions. It looked just as fearsome as the pictures of female African lions in her teacher's *National Geographics*.

A panther! They can swim, realized Irene. And it's not true they don't like water, not if there's a meal in it. In fact, one chased James Tilley's little brother last week. Irene felt sick. Her skin actually seemed to shrink right up the back of her neck. I never make the right decision, she fretted, thinking of the shotgun on the living-room wall. How would she get them all back safely to the house?

She rose to her knees and leaned toward the creek, holding the baby tightly.

"Homer," she called softly. "Homer, get here quick." The strain in her tone caught Homer's attention. "You be quiet and listen to me real good. There's a panther just the other bank, fixing to have us for dinner. You get the little ones out of there right now and don't make any fuss, you hear?"

"Sure, sure," Homer whispered back, the color draining out of his suntanned face.

Quickly the children began to scramble up the bank next to Irene. As they reached for their clothes, she called quietly to them.

"Just y'all start walking, right now! And don't look back or dawdle, and don't run either!"

"But we're nearly naked as jaybirds, Irene," complained Lucy.

"That much easier to swallow. Now get! I'll follow you and Homer. You both have to get the little ones up the road."

"I'll do it, Irene," said Homer quietly.

Irene turned her head to watch the panther as the children started up the road. He'd come out from the brush and was staring intently at the group. He seemed to be selecting a favorite. His ribs were sticking out and Irene could see his fangs as he licked his dry lips. As the panther began to slink across the creek, he managed to take a drink while continuing to stare at Irene and Baby Annie. Irene grabbed the shawl and followed the children. Now I've really done it, she thought. One shot would have scared him off. She could hear Lottie Mae crying and little Edward sniffling.

"He's going to eat us all," whimpered Edward.

"I won't let him, Edward," whispered Irene in reply. "Just you keep walking."

"But my legs won't move, Irene!"

Lucy grabbed Edward's arm and practically lifted him off the ground.

"I'll help you," she said firmly.

Robert was pulling Lottie Mae by the hand as they slowly approached the first bend. Irene walked with her head sideways to keep an eye behind her. She couldn't remember—was she supposed to be quiet or make a lot of noise? The panther was creeping up their side of the bank, near the pile of clothing. Pausing, he put his nose into the pile and sniffed. Like a cat with a toy he pushed them around and lifted his head with a puzzled look, mouth slightly open. Irene could swear he was smiling. A flush of heat passed through her body as she suddenly got angry.

"Smell tasty, do we? Can't decide who to eat first? I'll be doggone if you'll get a one!" As the panther began to stalk them, Irene grabbed some biscuits from her mother's apron pocket and threw them near the cat.

"Smell those!" she hissed.

While he gulped them down, the group gained a few precious feet. Again the panther started following, and Irene reached into the other pocket and threw the contents of the baby's bottle into the dust. The panther sniffed and kept coming.

We're so far away from our Homeplace, Irene worried frantically. And he's so close. Irene struggled to think straight.

"Walk farther apart," she ordered the children. Irene could see the big cat staring right at the baby when she turned. She threw the baby's shawl onto the road behind her, which made the panther stop short and sniff. He seemed to like this more than the biscuits. Now Irene was even more worried. She felt sweaty and cold at the same time. Rounding the bend with the baby starting to cry, Irene twisted her arm around herself and untied her apron, wiggling out of it while balancing Baby Annie. She let it fall to the ground without losing a step. Almost immediately the cat was upon it. Another pause from the panther, but not as long as the first. She threw her bonnet off to one side, then the baby's to the other side. The panther certainly liked the baby's clothes better. Irene yanked at her own dress, ripping the buttons apart as she pulled it off with one hand and threw it down.

The panther was watching every move. Having the children walk farther apart seemed to confuse him. Another precious few yards. He began to stalk Irene and the baby again, low to the ground, his powerful muscles rippling, his tongue licking his cheeks.

"There's the house," cried Edward. It squatted at the far edge of the wilted cotton field, the white-washed clapboard shining like a beacon. Irene could see the screen door of the washing porch and her parents' bedroom window.

"Homer," called Irene, "take Baby Annie and hold her tight, she's squirmy." She quickly gave the baby to Homer while they walked. "Homer," she continued, "cut across the field and keep walking fast as you can and don't let anyone stop for anything, no matter what!"

"We're never going to make it, Irene, he's right behind us," replied Homer.

"Hush up and do what I tell you, Homer Hardy. You're next oldest and you have to. When you get near the gate, y'all run and shut the door and windows fast, y'hear?"

"But Irene," whined Edward, still being propelled along by Lucy.

"Get moving," said Homer threateningly, keeping the pace as he stepped into the dry black dirt of the field. "Irene knows what she's doing." Irene and Homer exchanged a steady look.

"You be careful now, Irene," he cautioned. "Y'all watch those furrows—don't trip!" he whispered to the others as they followed him obediently.

"I'll be right behind y'all," she said as firmly as she could muster. She took a deep breath and turned around abruptly, planting her feet wide apart. The panther had started to trot and was taken aback by her move. "Look them straight in the eye, don't let them see you scared, and try to look real big," Daddy had said. Irene talked to herself loudly for courage as much as to frighten the panther.

"Hey!" she yelled sharply. "Hey, scaredy cat!" She waved her arms wildly over her head.

The panther was so surprised he stopped short and sat back on his haunches, as if she'd slapped him on the nose like a naughty house cat. He tilted his head quizzically. Slowly Irene reached down for the hem of her slip and flopped it back and forth like a piece of yarn. Fascinated, the cat followed her motions with a slight back-and-forth movement of his head. She began to sing in a firm, loud voice, all the while dancing backward at a brisk pace, kicking her legs out as far and as high as possible. Gradually she lifted her slip over her head. She zigzagged backward quickly through the field, keeping an eye on the panther through the slip armhole. She had reached the wagon path at the far edge of the field. Just as he began to wiggle as cats do before they spring, she balled up her slip and threw it as far as she could toward the panther. The cat pounced. Irene had already turned and started walking with a determined pace toward the house. She couldn't tell if she was hearing her own panting or the panther breathing behind her. As she reached the yard, she could see the nearby back door and screen-porch door open a crack and faces pressed against the closed back bedroom window. She took off for that crack in the door as if she'd been shot from a cannon, and Homer slammed it shut fast behind her as she barged into the bedroom. Suddenly she was covered with arms and legs and crying, shouting children.

"You saved us, Irene!" cried Edward.

"How'd you ever figure to do that dance, Irene? I'd never have been so smart." Lucy stared at her older sister in awe. "It's a good thing it's you that's the oldest."

"Look at that!" cried Lottie Mae from near the window. They looked out and saw the big cat shredding Irene's slip. His paw was holding it down as if it were a wounded animal, and he had a piece stuck on one fang as he arched his powerful head upward.

Irene leaned closer to the window with her arms around her brothers and sisters, trying to hug them all to her at once.

"Ha!" she shouted at the panther. "Just my old slip!" Irene was sure the panther stared at her for a moment, as if to be able to recognize her the next time.

"Irene," said Edward, with some of his usual bravado, "you're nearly naked as a jaybird, too."

"Well, I declare, Edward," replied Irene as she planted a kiss on his plump little cheek. "I guess we'll just have to tell Mama and Daddy it was too hot for clothes today."

"Yep," said Homer, grinning at Irene, the color now back in his face. "Hot as Hades!"

The Wish

"Grandpa Hutto is going to have your hide for drinking again, E.B." Irene peered through the barn's darkness and stared down at her lanky older cousin sprawled in the straw, leaning against the grain sacks. His hair was so close in color to the straw, it was hard to tell the difference.

E.B. fixed her with a glassy blue-eyed smirk. "Not if you don't tell him, squirt."

"You're no fun anymore, E.B. I'm going back to our game. C'mon, get up, you used to like hide 'n seek."

E.B. stroked his fuzzy blond mustache. "That's a stupid game. What're you now, eleven or twelve?"

Irene ignored his question. "It's not any more stupid than sitting on a scratchy old burlap sack drinking beer till you stink. You can sit here and drink yourself silly till Grandpa finds you, but I'm going to have some fun." She fixed him with a disgusted look and marched around to the front of the barn.

"Where's E.B., Irene?" asked Robert.

Irene rolled her eyes in response and jerked her head toward the back of the barn.

With his hands jammed in his pockets to steady himself, E.B. appeared and sauntered around to their game. With a loud belch he announced his presence.

"What y'all doin'?" he asked nonchalantly.

"Robert's 'It,' come 'n hide," shouted Homer.

"What a bunch of babies," he muttered just loud enough for Irene to hear. "There's almost as many small ones as chickens in the coop."

Irene looked down at E.B.'s bare, knobby ankles, noticing how much he'd grown out of his overalls. "Expecting a flood?" she asked pointedly, pleased to see she'd made him turn red. She turned away so she wouldn't have to smell his beer breath.

"One-two-three-four-five-six-seven-eight-nine-ten! Ready or not, here I come," shouted Robert, uncovering his eyes.

With a leap, E.B. followed Irene and landed behind the wagon next to her. He scrunched down. Irene tried to move away and still stay hidden.

"Poooh! You stink, E.B., get away!"

"So what?" replied E.B., moving in closer.

"You're a bigger pest than little Edward. Why don't you go bother Ruth over by the grown-ups? She says our game is dumb, too. You make a good pair of cousins; you can act obnoxious and she'll primp."

Robert's eager head popped up over the wagon edge. "I found you! I found two!"

They all took off for the home spot, Robert lunging ahead enthusiastically. "Ollie, Ollie, all come free! I won!" shouted Robert, tagging the tree.

Behind Robert, Irene suddenly whirled around and took a swing at E.B., who wobbled back as he laughed.

"Keep your paws off me!" she yelled. "I told you to get away! Now I'm going to go tell on you," she threatened, sticking her face as high up toward E.B.'s chin as she could.

"You do and you'll be sorry, squirt." He gave Irene a light shove, trying to cover his embarrassment over his voice coming out as a squeak.

"Then I'll tell," said Robert, coming over to stand protectively next to his sister. Even stretching his slight body, he was only up to Irene's shoulder.

E.B. leaned threateningly over Robert. "What if I held you upside down over the holding pond, huh? There was a mean old alligator in there last I looked." He flicked Robert's cowlick with his hand. Homer stepped in and put his arm around his younger brother, ready to take on E.B. if he had to.

"Why did we stop?" asked Edward, sidling up and tugging at Irene's trousers.

"Let's go play close to the house," said Irene, pulling Edward along.

"Why don't you go back where you crawled out of," shouted Robert as he caught up with Irene.

"Gotta hide behind a girl, Robert?" taunted E.B.

"I'm scared, Irene," whined Edward.

"E.B. is always making trouble," said Robert quietly. "I wish he'd stayed home. He's not a real close cousin, anyway."

"E.B.'s all right, Robert, that's his beer talking. Don't worry, Edward, he won't dare make trouble near Grandpa." She patted him gently on his head. "Race!" she called out. With Irene leading, they ran toward the circle of light near the back screen door, Lottie Mae and Lucy trailing behind as usual. They arrived in a jumble at the card table.

"Whoa!" called Grandpa Hutto. "Watch the kerosene lamps! Someone'll get hurt. We're trying to have a game of cards here. Thought y'all were supposed to play by the barn."

Ruth barely glanced in their direction from her blanket, except to bat her eyelashes at the air.

"E.B.'s being mean, Grandpa," said Irene, with a defiant glance back at E.B., who had followed the group.

Grandpa Hutto made an ominous noise in his throat. "E.B., you've been warned before. You ought to have better sense. You best help these children get the BB guns loaded and you can all go clean out those mice from the grain barn." He turned to Daddy. "What do you say, son, five cents' bounty apiece?" Daddy gave a nod. "Now leave us some peace and quiet, it's not every day we get to have your grandma and grandpa Haskell stay over here at our Homeplace, or your aunt Belle and uncle Joseph."

"Ruth," added Grandpa Haskell, "I don't suppose you'd quit your lollygaggin' about and join your cousins?"

"Daddy!" hissed Mama. "Lola said leave her be.

She's a young lady now. It's a wonder Lola got her to come with Belle at all."

Grandpa Haskell made a disapproving "Humpf!" and held the cards alongside his face so Ruth couldn't hear. "Your sister's letting that girl lead her by the nose," he stated. He turned his attention toward E.B. "Go on about your business, boy!"

E.B. knew better than to argue with either of Irene's grandfathers or her father.

"C'mon," called E.B. with a sigh. As he led the way toward the screen door, he took care to leave a generous distance between the adults and himself.

"Look who thinks he's so big," muttered Robert.

"It's just to keep him busy," whispered Irene.

E.B. reached up to the wall rack and handed each of the older children a gun and some BBs.

"Let's go, slowpokes." He sneered, punching open the screen door and continuing down the steps without a backward glance. "I bet Charley's not really doing chores, just making me do his big-brother dirty work."

"I don't remember him being so mean," commented Lucy softly, carrying her gun with one hand

and hanging on to her constant shadow, Lottie Mae, with the other.

"Don't pay him any mind," whispered Irene to the others as they all went back across the barnyard to the grain barn and sat down to load.

"Darn," cussed Irene, "I can never get these old BBs down the barrel."

"Here, Irene," said E.B., coming over to sit next to her. "I'll show you how."

Irene didn't like him sitting so close. If he hadn't smelled so bad, she wouldn't have known he was tipsy. He almost sounded like his old self.

"Stupid girl," he muttered as he fed the BBs into her gun.

Moron, thought Irene.

All seven of the cousins balanced quietly on the grain barn's inside wooden ledge. They were perched a few feet above the grain pile, in the dark. Irene tried not to get squirmy while remembering to keep her gun pointed down. The children knew if they waited, the mice would forget they were there. Sure enough, they began to hear the mice scampering across the pile. E.B. switched on the single lightbulb. The five children fired at once. Lottie Mae and Edward clapped their hands over their ears and squealed with excitement. Everyone jumped down and reached for the four bodies to show Grandpa and Daddy.

"You carry mine, Homer," ordered Irene.

"What's the matter, squirt, scared of a little mouse?" E.B. was at it again.

"I don't mind shooting 'em. I just don't like to touch anything all mushed up dead."

They marched back toward the card players, each trying to claim responsibility for killing a mouse. E.B. started waving his in front of Irene, saying, "Look at all the mush, Irene, how about some supper?"

Irene looked the other way and Homer moved in between them. They arrived at the card table and Grandpa Hutto gave Robert their twenty-cents reward.

"Y'all have to split it," he said. "I can't stand this squabbling over who gets what. Now go unload those BB guns and put them away, and get rid of the mice."

Ruth had turned her back to the group and was inspecting her fingernails as if she were a model.

When the boys ran off with their mice, E.B.

glanced at Irene and snuck behind her as they were walking.

"Tattletale," he hissed.

Irene decided not to pop him one, he was too big. And he still had that bloody mouse by the tail. She could smell it behind her, along with E.B.'s disgusting breath. She walked a little faster. She felt a tug as something fell down the back of her blouse.

"Ha!" shouted E.B. "Let's see you get that out! He's too mushed up to get ahold of!"

For one second Irene was too horrified to move. She could feel a warm dampness spreading down her back. She could smell a barn smell and feel fur and the hard rubbery tail twisting against her skin. It was E.B.'s dead mouse! She screamed and frantically tried to lift her shirt over her head. Wriggling, she cussed E.B. at the top of her lungs. Irene ran in a circle and struggled to reach her back and pull the shirt away, but it was stuck fast at the waistband of her trousers.

"Mama! Daddy! Grandpa! Homer! Help! Get it off me, it's all over me, get it off me!" She squirmed every which way at once, clutching first over her shoulder, then under her arms, trying to get that mushed-up dead mouse out of her shirt, looking for all the world like she was having a fit. The children gathered around her, too shocked to help.

"HEYYYYY!" It was a sound more like a roar than a shout, followed by Grandpa Hutto running so fast he seemed like a tornado. The rest of the adults were close behind. The children backed away in a circle, leaving poor Irene in the middle and E.B. doubled up with his back to Grandpa, laughing and slapping his knee. For a split second there was that type of calm and electricity in the air, like before you're hit by a storm, when your hair stands up all over. Grandpa looked at the bloody, lumpy back of Irene's shirt and at E.B. He grabbed E.B. and picked him right up in the air and yelled in his face.

"Get out of my sight! And don't you dare leave the farm until I'm done with you!" He dropped him like a sack of grain. It seemed as though he grabbed Irene at the same time with his other arm and yanked that mouse right out of her shirt. Irene had her eyes squeezed shut so tight she didn't even realize Grandpa was carrying her back to the house, the other adults following.

"Now you calm down, Li'l Bit," he said soothingly as they entered the kitchen and he sat her on the table. "The mouse is gone and so is E.B. I'll take care of him later, you can rest yourself about that! Right now we'll take off this shirt and clean you up." He opened the spigot and let some water into the kitchen pail and picked up a rag. "There's not much here, anyway," he said. "It's not as bad as you think." He rinsed out the rag and washed Irene's face as she gulped and tentatively opened her eyes.

"I hope he dies," she said, with all the fury she felt. "I hope someone big mushes him up real good and he dies!"

"Now, Irene, I know he did a mean thing, but just because E.B.'s been wicked, we still don't wish him dead. I'm gonna talk to E.B. He won't pull a stunt like this again, you believe me! And remember, that was still just a mouse, even if it was dead and a little bloody. You've killed snakes and mice before."

Irene looked up at Grandpa, not quite convinced. But she knew she didn't have to worry about E.B. again. Absolutely no one wanted to make Grandpa Hutto angry. He was the biggest man in the family and still had the last word on everything important. E.B. was just lucky Grandpa never lifted a finger against anyone, thought Irene. Grandpa's thick handlebar mustache could make him look even more ferocious.

"Now you go get a clean blouse and a glass of lemonade from your mother. You scared her half to death with all that screaming."

"That's the truth," said Mama as she went over to the icebox to chip off some ice for the lemonade.

E.B.'s mother, Sarah, clasped her hands tightly against her chest. "I just don't understand what's gotten into that boy lately, Mae," she fretted.

By the time dinner was over, everyone was back to normal, except Irene. She could still feel that squishy lump. She hadn't gone very far from her mother's side since she'd seen Grandpa stride off toward the barn. Homer had said he'd never seen him so scary as when he picked up E.B. That made Irene feel better, but as she fell asleep that night she had to sleep on her stomach.

It seemed just a moment had passed to Irene; she had to think why the sun would be up when she'd just gone to bed. Then she remembered the day before, jumped up and shook herself, scratching her back as if she had a batch of ringworm. As Irene headed toward the kitchen, she heard Cousin Sarah sobbing and her mother's voice saying something soothing. She peeked around the doorway.

Cousin Sarah was sitting at the kitchen table with her head in her hands. Between sobs she was saying, "I never should've let E.B. go off hunting this morning, he was probably still tipsy. It's so hard to tell when he's listening and when he's just going to go off and do something stupid."

Irene crept back from the kitchen door to listen to E.B.'s mother.

"His father's told him a hundred times to keep that safety on when he's walking around. How on earth can he have shot himself?"

Robert came up the other end of the hall, brown eyes big as saucers. "You killed him, Irene. I heard you say you wanted him to die. Now he's gone and done it."

"That's not true, Robert, you can't wish someone dead. Anyway, how do you know he's dead?"

"Charley ran back from hunting and said E.B. shot himself when he tripped and was stuck under the barbed wire all mushed up dead. That's how, and you wished it!"

Irene thought she was going to be sick. She ran to her favorite place in the barn, the newborn calf's stall. She sat down next to him and let him suck her finger.

"God doesn't do what little kids say. Robert's just mad at me. Maybe God could be mad we shot his mice, but Grandpa says we're supposed to keep them from eating the grain." She looked into the calf's brown eyes. "Maybe he just wanted to prove he exists. Maybe he heard me say he was a mean God for letting your mama die and he's angry at me. Anyway, I didn't really mean to have him die, he was okay sometimes, and after all, he is, *was,* my cousin, even if he was mostly mean." Irene laid her head on the top of the calf's and tried not to cry. She wished she could think about something else. Irene heard the door open and saw her grandpa's feet as he began his chores. She curled down behind the calf as small as she could, but it didn't do any good. Grandpa Hutto always seemed to know when she was around.

Grandpa came over next to Irene and knelt down.

"Calf misses his mother, eh?"

"I think so," replied Irene quietly.

"It wasn't anybody's doing that his mother died when he was born, you know. We talked about that the other day, remember, Little Bit? Maybe we made a mistake not to get the vet, but it seemed like it was going to be a normal birth, and we manage all the time. Even so, it probably wasn't possible the vet could have helped. We tried our best."

Irene was quiet. She wanted to say she understood, but the words wouldn't come out.

"We can't make people die by wishing, Irene, no matter how wicked or mean they are. E.B. made a stupid mistake, he didn't think. He knew how he should have carried a gun and he was just too care-less to put the safety on."

Irene tried to believe this. It was hard to accept that E.B. could be gone forever over something so simple and so quick. When her grandma Hutto died, it was after she'd been sick a long while. Then she remembered what her sister Lucy had told her. Lucy was always reading about exotic places she was going to visit when she became a writer.

"Grandpa, Lucy says that way over in India they

believe if you die and you're not real bad you come back to life as something special, like a cow. You're not allowed to eat cows in India."

"Well, Irene," said Grandpa, "this isn't India and I don't know about that, but I've heard tell of it. I suppose anything is possible."

"Do you think E.B. would mind if we named the calf after him?"

Grandpa scooped up Irene in his strong arms and said, "Little Bit, I think E.B. and his mama would be real tickled by that."

The Fugitive

"Daddy, Daddy! There's someone down by the creek!" Irene gasped for breath as she stopped short of running smack into her father. "He's half naked sitting there, Daddy. He's got chains around his ankles!"

"What?" her father responded. "What's that?"

"A man, Daddy, a big man, with chains! He's covered in blood, and he's just sitting there."

Her father's lean body tensed visibly as he stopped working on the broken bench. He bounded up the porch steps, turning around at the door toward Irene.

"Get Thomas and Charley, they're down at the barn. Tell them come up to the house straightaway."

Irene flew across the narrow yard road past the smokehouse, her straight brown hair swinging from side to side, her bare feet barely touching the scorching dirt. Barreling into the shadows of the barn, she yelled her father's instructions to her older brother and the hired hand, Thomas. They dropped their tools and hurried out of the barn, Irene right behind them. As they ran past the dog pen, she shouted to Robert.

"Come on, there's a strange man all bloody with chains!"

Robert and Irene rushed up to the white-board farmhouse as their father emerged, the screen door slamming behind him.

"Take these guns, boys, Irene's seen someone, sounds like a convict, down by the creek. He's bleeding and his chains are still on. Let's go." He handed Charley and Thomas their guns and they took off at a quick pace toward the creek. "Mae," he yelled to Mama, "don't you worry." Irene and her younger brother were about to follow when Mama called from inside the house.

"Irene, Robert, you stay here," she commanded. Peering through the screen door, Irene could see her mother loading a shotgun. "As a matter of fact, you two get in here and round up the little ones. Take them into the back bedroom and stay there till I tell you to come out."

Mama looked even more dainty than usual with the big shotgun under her arm.

"What're you going to do, Mama?" asked Irene.

"This isn't the time for questions, honey. You mind now, and hurry. We'll be fine."

"Yes, ma'am, I'm hurrying," replied Irene as she tugged at Robert's sleeve to pull him along.

"Where's Lucy? She could help, too," complained Robert.

"She's out in back with Baby Annie. Go shout for them," ordered Irene. "I'll find Homer and Edward."

The children crowded into the living room. Irene shepherded them into the bedroom with its view of the yard road.

"Irene, why do we have to be in here? It's not nap time," whined Lottie Mae. "I need to go to the outhouse." Her doll-like features threatened to turn into a pout.

"Look, Mama said to stay in here. I saw an escaped convict down by the creek and Daddy's gone to get him. Now stop complaining, you'll just have to wait."

"A convent?" asked little Edward. "What's a convent?"

"Not a convent, dummy," said Robert. "A convict! Someone who's locked up in jail because he's dangerous."

Irene stared out the window, squinting against the bright Texas sun to see through the haze. In the yard the mesquite trees appeared to shimmy in the heat waves. The creek was hidden across the field and around the bend behind the house, but she wanted to be sure to catch a first glimpse of whatever was going to happen.

"I think they're coming!" exclaimed Irene.

All seven of the children crowded around the window.

"It's them, all right. See, the one in the middle is stumbling, they're holding him!" she said.

"Here they come! He's so big, Irene, do you think he can break loose?" Lottie Mae hid behind Irene, peeking out.

Edward pushed in front of Irene and Lottie Mae, not wanting to miss a thing.

"Let me see, Lottie. Just 'cause I'm littler, you don't have to hog the window." Standing on his tiptoes, he put his chin on the windowsill and managed to look out into the yard. "He's bloody! What a mean man!" bellowed little Edward.

"Listen to those chains, listen to him dragging those chains," whispered Homer. "I bet he has to be pretty strong to've broken those off."

The ankle chains rattled and scraped along the ground as the big man shuffled between Thomas and Charley. When they reached the truck, Irene could see Thomas help the convict gently into the back and climb up next to him. Daddy got into the driver's seat and started the truck as Charley stood back.

"We'll be back by dinnertime, Mae," he yelled to Mama. Within moments only a cloud of dust was left in the yard.

Irene led the pack of children as they scrambled out of the bedroom through the washing porch and rushed into the front room to find their mother.

"We think it's Horace Mooney," Charley was saying as the children entered. "They're taking him back over there and are going to make sure he's secured."

"Charley, are they taking him back to jail?" asked Robert.

"Did he fight real hard? Were you afraid?" asked Homer. "What did Daddy do?"

Charley looked to his mother for help, as he lifted both of their shotguns up to the wall rack.

"Children," she replied, "Horace Mooney isn't a convict. He's going home to his family. He didn't hurt anyone, he's only confused. Stumbling through the brush lost all day, poor thing. His mother is probably worried sick. I'm sure Charley was real brave, too."

"Well, I was scared at first. He didn't want to get up and he tried to shove Daddy. But then he looked real scared himself."

"He's not a convict?" lamented Homer. "Gee, I thought it was going to be real exciting."

"That was quite enough excitement for today, Homer. Horace isn't mean, just not right in the head. Now I'm going back to my chores. It's almost supper time and a family still has to eat," said Mama.

"Why did he have those heavy chains around his legs if he's not a convict?" asked Homer, trailing after his mother.

"Well, sometimes people aren't born right and they do things that might hurt themselves or someone else. His people try to keep him safe. You'll understand more when you're older," she said. Mama retreated into the pantry and called, "Who wants chicken and biscuits for supper?"

"I do!"

"Me, too!"

"Can we save some for Ring? It's his favorite and he always eats those old dog scraps," Robert pleaded in his most pathetic voice.

"That old coon dog likes rabbits the best, Robert," interrupted Lucy, looking up from writing furiously in her diary.

"What d'you know, Lucy? You're always in dream-land with some book. It's a waste of time anyway, girls can't be writers."

"They can, too! If you'd ever read a book instead of listening to Homer all the time, you'd know."

"There won't be anything for anyone unless we get the table set and the supper made," replied Mama. "Girls, one of you come over here and mix up the biscuits while I go out and get a chicken. Then we can finish the gravy. Robert, you climb up and check the water level. It's a nice breezy day, so you can turn on the windmill and fill up the tank. But don't go wandering off and forget to cut off the spigot."

Irene started to plead for a turn to climb up the tank, then decided today she'd rather help Mama. One day I'd like to know how to rig up a windmill pump like Daddy and Grandpa, she thought. Climbing up the connecting pipes to the holding tank over the house was like being in a tree, only better, since it was higher than most trees around their place. When Mama opened the spigot in the kitchen or the windmill was turned on and pumped water out of the ground into the tank, Irene could hear it rushing through the high pipes. She couldn't wait until Daddy put a spigot in the bathroom, too, so they wouldn't have to carry pails of heated water out to the washing-porch bathtub room.

The children scattered to do their chores and Irene went to start the biscuits. She loved using her grandmother's old tan mixing bowl. Soon she'd be able to reach it without standing on the apple crate.

She lined up the flour, the shortening, the baking powder, and the milk in front of her. She had a rhyme in her head for the recipe to make it easier to remember. She was glad she had to concentrate on it so she didn't have to keep thinking about Horace Mooney.

Two cups flour,
with three teaspoons baking powder,
not fish chowder.

One-half teaspoon salt, or it'll be my fault.
Mix it up dry, don't ask me why.
Now cut in one-half cup shortening, chop a lot
so it looks like oatmeal, only it's not.
Don't forget, almost one cup milk.
Stir and pat and roll and cut out.
Bake it hot and give a shout.
Now they're done and that is that.
Eat too many and you'll get fat.

Irene still hadn't figured out how to include "place in a hot oven and bake for ten to fifteen minutes."

Mama came back holding the headless chicken. She held a pail of water in one hand and the twitching body in the other.

Homer sidled over to Irene and stuck his finger in the dough.

"James Tilley said Horace Mooney got loose one time and killed Old Lady Flynn's chickens with his bare hands," he whispered. "He saw the whole mess himself. I just never knew who Horace Mooney was."

"Homer! Mother! Homer's telling stories again! Get your smelly finger out of the dough, go away!"

"Homer," Mama reprimanded, "how many times

have I told you to stop pestering Irene? Now get on about your business and go feed those mules. You can fetch some more wood for the stove on your way back—I'm going to need more hot water to finish cleaning this bird." The odor of burning chicken feathers filled the room as Mama singed the ends of the pinfeathers stuck in the skin.

Irene and Mama worked side by side at the stove as they made gravy.

"You have to cook the flour and lard a little longer, honey, until it gets nice and brown from the fat. Just keep on stirring, be patient."

"Mama, do you think they let Horace Mooney eat with the rest of the family?"

"Irene, I don't know. It probably depends on how he behaves and if they can control him."

"What do you think he might do?" Irene persisted. "Would he turn over the table or play in his food? Do you think he uses silverware?"

Mama put more wood in the fire and another pot of water on the burner. She wiped her cheek with a sigh.

"Young lady, that's enough. You always have a hundred questions and now you're about to burn that gravy till even the pigs won't eat it. There's no way I can know the answer to those things and it's none of our business. There's more important things you and I have to talk about, like tomorrow. Daddy and I have to go over to the one hundred sixty field in Taft to check how things are going, and Grandpa's going to visit a friend. He won't be home till after you're all asleep. Honey, see to it that everyone does their chores. We'll be back next day, so you'll have to make sure the little ones get cleaned up and in bed, too. Charley and Thomas are coming with us to help with the heavy work."

"What about Homer? He always gives me trouble about doing his chores."

"You don't have to worry about Homer tomorrow. He's going to be at Mr. Connors's all day helping him."

Irene sighed. Mama put an arm around her and gave her a hug. "I know, Irene, but you are the oldest next to Charley, and it's your place to help. Since Thomas moved into the old bunkhouse and started as our hired hand, it's been a bit easier on Charley. Now he gets more time for his studies. Pretty soon

Lucy and the five other little ones will be bigger and it'll be easier on you and me both. I sure am glad I can count on you when I have to be away. Open the oven door, honey, so I can put the bird in, or we'll never get this dinner on the table."

"Well, this time you better warn the boys not to tease me. Homer and Robert always start trouble and nobody minds me. Then I get blamed."

"I'll take care of it, Irene, don't worry. Daddy will talk to him."

Irene rolled her eyes. She knew how much good that would do once her parents had left the farm.

The sound of the truck in front of the house caught everyone's attention.

"Get this table set, girls, Daddy's back. You know how he likes dinner to be on time," said Mama.

The next morning as Homer was using the old hickory tree stump to mount his horse, Irene rushed out the back door and yelled, "Don't forget to come straight back after dinner! I don't want to stay up half the night worrying about you!"

"What's the matter, Irene, you afraid to be here alone with the little ones? Woooo! Better watch out or the boogeyman will get you, sneak up on you and get you!" Homer dug his heels into his horse and was across the yard as Irene yelled again.

"I'm telling if you don't come back on time!"

"Yeah, yeah, I'll do whatever I want, I may even stay overnight!"

"Don't you dare," shouted Irene to Homer's depart-ing back. She kicked the ground and stomped into the house.

That evening Lucy held the lamp up between her and Irene. The flickering kerosene lamp cast an eerie glow around her red curls.

"Irene, do you think there's enough kerosene?"

Irene was worried something might happen to the Delco lights in the ceiling. She knew the bulbs ran from a wire connected to batteries Daddy had rigged up in the shed. She sure enough wasn't going to count on them tonight. Especially when only Charley and the men knew how to start the gas motor to charge them.

"Maybe you should go fill it up," Irene replied.

"You go get it. You're in charge. It's already dark outside," said Lucy.

Irene hesitated. "I guess there's plenty to last us the night."

A coyote bayed in the distance. From the dog pen Ring howled in response. Irene shivered. Lucy watched her big sister and then glanced around the room at the shadows.

"Are all the doors locked?" Lucy asked.

"Let's check. You start with the washing porch behind Mama and Daddy's bedroom and I'll start in the kitchen."

"No, you start with the porch, Irene."

"Let's just do it together," replied Irene, taking Lucy's hand. Irene had never noticed how every room opened onto a porch. At least the two back bedrooms opened onto the screened washing porch, with a door they could lock.

"What do you suppose is taking Homer so long?" Irene wondered out loud to Lucy. "Let's bring everyone into Mama and Daddy's bedroom. Get the quilts and we'll make pallets on the floor."

Lottie Mae started to complain as soon as they

tried to move her from her bed. "I want to sleep in my own bed with my doll, Irene!" Her cherubic face began to crumple as sudden tears welled in her big blue eyes.

"Well, I want to tell everyone a fairy tale and it's easier this way," said Irene. "You can bring your doll and she can listen." Irene really wished Homer would return. It was just like him to stick her with all the work. She glanced out the window and noticed there was hardly any moonlight tonight. She couldn't even see the outline of the barn.

While Lucy settled the children, Irene dashed to the kitchen and returned, hiding a butcher knife under her skirt just as Lucy turned around.

"Irene!" Lucy came over quickly and whispered, "What're you doing with that knife? You're not strong enough to stab anybody."

"No, but I could cut the screens so we could get out of here if we had to! I'm going to bring the shotgun in here, too," she said, hurrying out of the room.

Irene returned and placed the loaded gun in the corner away from the children.

"Okay, let's start the story," she stated, staring back at the children's awed faces.

"Tell a cowboy and Indian story, Irene," pleaded little Edward.

"No, a princess one," cried Lottie Mae.

"This is about both," began Irene. Lucy rolled her eyes, her writer's senses appalled.

The children fell asleep before Irene had to invent much of a story. Lucy and Irene were left in the lengthening shadows listening for Homer's return. The coyote bayed again, this time closer to the house. The girls waited for Ring's response.

"Why doesn't Ring howl?" asked Lucy. "He always howls back."

From the other side of the room Robert sat up, clutching his blanket under his chin.

"Do you think he's okay?" he asked. "The coyote didn't seem that close, did he?"

"Do you think he's near the coop?" Lucy sounded worried.

"No, the fence is too high and Daddy covered the top, anyway," replied Irene. "He'd have to have hands to open the gate. And coyotes aren't that smart." Irene was fairly certain, anyway.

No sooner had Irene replied than they heard the most gosh-awful commotion from the chickens.

Squeaking and squawking like they were in a frenzy. Lucy and Irene sat bolt upright and grabbed each other's hands.

"What if it's that crazy man wringing all their necks?" whimpered Lucy.

"Irene!" whispered Robert. "You better go out there and scare him off with that gun!"

"Don't be silly, you know they chained him up." I hope, thought Irene, as she reassured the others.

"He got away before! Oh, Irene, I'm so scared! Where is that stupid Homer? He should be back by now." Lucy dug both hands into her thick auburn hair and dramatically clutched her head.

"Probably taking his own sweet time just to be pesky. Anyway, a lot of help he'd be." Irene reached for her sister's hand and listened for the chickens, who were now quiet. Too quiet, thought Irene.

"Irene, what about Ring? I still don't hear him barking." Robert was clearly worried, leaning forward to hear the slightest sound.

They all sat quietly, waiting. And then they heard it. It was their worst fear come to life. The sound of a rattling chain moving across the ground. Their ears followed the sound as it slowly moved around the house. They all gasped as the back porch door creaked.

"I thought we locked that door!" Irene whispered.

"I could swear we did," said Lucy with a trembling lip. "He must have just ripped it open! Oh, no! I bet he killed all the chickens. What are you going to do, Irene? You have to do something!"

"Do you think Ring's okay?" asked Robert in a muffled voice. He was shivering under his blanket.

"Hush! Let me think. Lucy, you wake the kids and go over by the window. Here, take the knife. Be ready to slit the screen and jump out. If you have to run, stay by the side toward the front of the house and then go straight to the road where Homer should be coming back, and flag him down so he can ride for help. Don't go out until I tell you or you'll get attacked."

Irene crept across the floor and grabbed the shotgun. She unlocked the safety, tucked it under her chin, and planted her feet apart opposite the sound. They could hear the chains dragging on the wooden porch. Scrape a little and rattle. Scrape and then rattle.

In a barely audible voice Irene called, "Who's

there?" She gulped and shouted with more confidence. "You better speak up and tell me who you are!"

The scrape and rattle came closer.

Over her shoulder Irene motioned to Lucy to be ready. Lucy held the knife against the screen, the children cowering around her.

"This is your last chance and I'm not kidding! Speak up!"

No response.

"I'm going to shoot straight through this wall!" Before she knew it, a huge ragged hole appeared in the wall. Just as she was ready to empty the other barrel, a howl of indignation erupted through the fist-sized hole into the bedroom.

"You winged me! You're going to be in big trouble, Irene! Mama and Daddy will kill you for this hole!"

Irene couldn't believe it. For a moment she thought she might faint. Then she was furious.

"Kill me? Homer Hardy, you are the stupidest boy ever! It's your own fault for such a dumb joke. It's a wonder you're not deader than a doornail!"

Lucy's arm was still raised with the knife against the screen, her mouth hanging open. Robert and the others stared wide-eyed through the hole at their older brother.

Holding his arm, he leaned his head against the hole and peered into the bedroom. "It's a good thing you're such a bad shot, Irene." He gave a pained smirk, but he was beginning to look pale in spite of himself.

"You don't have the sense God gave Ring, Homer," said Lucy, dropping her arm with the knife. She marched out of the room with her shoulders back and called in as haughty a tone as she could muster, "Homer, I'll get the iodine and bandages, but next time you may not have such fool luck!"

Irene stood rooted to the spot. Automatically she lowered the shotgun, pointing it toward the floor. In a slow, steady voice she announced, "Anybody tells Mama and Daddy how this hole got in the wall and you'll have to answer to me!"

The Hunt

"It's not fair, a men's hunt."

"Irene, enough of this foolishness," said Mama. "We'll talk about this after the men leave. Robert, get on that truck before Daddy runs out of patience with you and those noisy dogs. Now, you do what the men tell you and have a good time." She gave Robert a hug and pushed him gently down the porch steps toward the pickup.

Irene glared at Daddy in the driver's seat.

"Those dogs go more places than me."

"Bye, 'Rene," called Robert from the back of the truck, not quite brave enough to look her in the eye.

Irene ignored Robert's good-bye and Daddy's wave.

"Mama," complained Irene, "I—"

"Watch your mouth, Missy. There are some things you can't do. Come on, let's go inside and get our chores done. Maybe we'll have time for a game of solitaire." Mama went into the kitchen, Irene so close behind her the screen door didn't get a chance to squeak.

"I want to do something different, Mama."

"We all do, honey, but women don't go on these coon hunts."

"Robert couldn't shoot a raccoon if it came up to him and said 'Howdy,'" Irene grumbled softly.

While Irene was still muttering about life being unfair to girls, the bouncing truck was sliding Robert from one side of the truck bed to the other, along with all the yelping dogs.

"Ring," he said, gripping his dog tightly around the neck, "we finally got to go on a hunt! We'll be there soon, boy. Quit your slobbering and look snappy. See all these other hounds?" The truck bumped along the dirt road deeper into the woods along the river. Finally Daddy slowed down enough for the dogs to get a firm footing and their barking became even more frantic. Ring picked up the anticipation and danced around Robert as the truck came to a halt.

"Robert," called Daddy, "get those dogs off the truck, but watch you don't get all tangled while you tie them up." Daddy started unloading the guns, checking each safety as he leaned them against a tree, while he said hello to his friends.

"Hey, Robert! About time you and that dog of yours got here. What's been holding you up?"

Robert grinned at his uncle Norm, glad to feel welcomed. He unhitched the back and the dogs leapt out, joining his uncle Norm's pack, sniffing introductions. Ring held back, eager to be included but nervous about the reception.

"Don't worry, boy." Robert walked over to the edge of the commotion to pet his agitated dog. "You'll do fine. They'll all want you to come every time when they find out what a great nose you have. Just follow ol' Traveler there, he's supposed to be the best hunting dog ever, got the best nose for tracking raccoons in the county. All you got to do is find 'em and chase 'em up a tree for us. That's not so hard, is it, boy?" Robert gathered up the dogs and tried to tell them to be patient, but they knew why they'd come and were eager to begin the hunt.

Someone called, "Okay, let them go!" All the dogs took off, barking furiously, with Ring enthusiastically bringing up the rear. Robert watched them until they were out of sight.

"Time's a wasting," said Uncle Norm. "Let's set up camp near the river," he called as he started down the trail.

The sun was disappearing as the last blankets were folded into pallets and spread out around the fire. The fragrant smoke from the mesquite fire stung Robert's eyes but he didn't want to move away from the men and the warmth.

"Aren't we going to follow the dogs?" he asked the group.

"Nope. We'll sit here and listen. When they get one treed we'll go."

"Robert, come over here and sit next to me." Uncle Norm patted the pallet at his side. "The smoke isn't blowing this way. Your pa's sure lucky to have four boys to take hunting. Not that my gals Ruth and Ruby ain't fine young women, but it ain't the same thing." He gave Robert an enthusiastic clap on the back.

"What happens if the dogs get lost?" asked Robert nervously. Some of the men chuckled, startling Robert.

"Heck, they're hunting dogs, they can smell their way home, boy."

Robert hoped Ring stayed with the pack and didn't wander off to look for him. Maybe he'd better not ask any more questions; it might embarrass Daddy to have him seem so ignorant about hunting. Still, he thought, how'm I supposed to find out if I don't ask?

The men started in on stories about past hunts and about the biggest, oldest, smartest coon in this part of Texas.

"Remember when Charley almost had Ol' Diablo?"

"Yeah, but it was even better the night Henry heard him following right behind us."

"By golly, his tracks were bigger than any coon I ever saw!" remarked Daddy.

Robert felt bold enough to add his two cents. "James Tilley said he saw him drag their dinner right off the campfire! He was gone before anyone could move."

Daddy beamed at Robert and gave him a resounding clap on the shoulder. "I'd believe that, wouldn't you, boys?" he asked. "He would be a prize, yes sir."

The men nodded and chuckled and settled down on their pallets, drinking coffee with unself-conscious slurping. Robert took a manly swig of Mama's root beer and began to feel as if he'd been coming on hunts forever.

The stars came out and filled the night sky. A hoot owl called in the distance and still the men continued to tell stories. Robert could hear the dogs howling. In spite of his excitement, he was beginning to feel sleepy from the warmth of the fire and the long day. He moved closer to his father.

"Daddy," he whispered.

"What, son?"

"When do we follow the dogs?"

"Well, it doesn't sound like they've turned up anything interesting yet."

"How can you tell?"

"You get to know by the sound of their bark."

Robert listened intently, trying to hear over the noise of the men laughing at some joke he didn't understand.

"Daddy, I think they're tracking it back this way!"

"Could be. You can never be sure till they get here."

The root beer Robert had drunk was having its effect.

"I have to go, Daddy."

"Go where, son? Oh, I get it. Go down by the river and pick a spot."

"Don't fall in, boy. Garfish feed at night," teased one of the men.

Robert moved hesitantly out of the friendly firelight, stumbling over something in the dark.

"You all right, Robert?" he heard his father call.

"Yeah." He continued toward the sound of the water. It's creepy out here in the dark, he thought. Bet Irene would be scared silly.

"Crickets making noises and there goes that spook owl calling to the bats." Robert spoke softly to himself and felt better hearing the sound of a voice, even his own.

Something brushed his cheek. He jumped and then scolded himself for acting like a girl. He could still hear the men and make out the glow of the fire through the trees. He unbuttoned his fly. Something was watching him, he was certain. The memory of the panther at the creek popped into his head. He held the waist of his pants with shaking hands. Very cautiously he looked around, fighting the urge to flee. Straining to see in the darkness, he turned his head forward and discovered two yellow eyes on the branch above him.

Robert tried to yell but his throat was paralyzed. The yellow eyes were locked with his own. Slowly, a shape was beginning to emerge from the shadows surrounding the glowing eyes.

Crunch! There was something behind him!

"Robert?" his father said. "What the heck is taking you—"

"Look," Robert croaked, pointing to the tree. The yellow eyes seemed to squint and take the measure of both figures.

"I'll be a son of a gun." Daddy let out a low whistle and ran back toward the fire, Robert close on his heels.

"Hey, y'all! Get down here, Robert treed the biggest granddaddy of them all, Ol' Diablo himself. Where are those fool dogs? Somebody whistle 'em in."

When Robert reached the campsite the men were scrambling around picking up their guns, struggling into their boots, and stumbling over the pallets in the dim light. They were making almost as much noise as the hounds, who were obviously out of whistle range. Robert picked up his gun and stood waiting impatiently, hopping from one foot to the other. Finally they followed Robert, tramping behind him through the brush as he ran ahead.

"He's gone! He was right here," Robert said dejectedly, pointing to the tree branch.

"Saw him with my own eyes," said Daddy.

"Sure must have been Ol' Diablo, he's not one to hang around," said one of the men.

"Sure is slick, that ol' coon," commented Uncle Norm.

"Robert, that was him. No other coon would've come so close. Well, fellas, might as well go back and finish our coffee and wait for the dogs to come in."

"But won't the dogs track him?" asked Robert.

"Nah, they'll be plumb tuckered out."

"But Daddy—" began Robert.

"C'mon with the men, Robert," interrupted Daddy. "I'm real proud of you, son. You're probably the only man of us to see that coon so close up. And on your first hunt, too." Daddy put one arm around Robert's shoulder and carried his shotgun with the other, heading back toward the fire.

Puzzled, Robert copied Daddy's hold on the gun and tried to figure out why his father was so proud. If he hadn't drunk so much root beer, he never would have seen the coon. He didn't look that much bigger than a normal coon. Guess I was just too scared to notice in the dark, he decided.

The dogs came staggering back into the campsite with their tongues hanging down to their knees. Some of them flopped right down on the pallets. Uncle Norm shooed them off. "Get up off there, you worthless hounds! You lazy things missed the action. We're thinking about giving Robert your job from now on!"

Robert moved closer to Daddy and whispered, "Did you ever get a coon, Daddy?"

"Well now, we just came real close, didn't we, son! I think that's about it for tonight, must be after midnight. We'll get him next time. Robert, you put our dogs on the truck and I'll get Mama's coffeepot and the guns." Daddy moved away to pick up the guns and Robert was left with no choice but to collect the dogs.

Come to think of it, he didn't remember anyone ever actually bringing home anything from a hunt.

The Race

The next morning Robert was late getting to breakfast. Irene was waiting at the table.

"Don't see you dragging any coons, smarty-pants. Not even a poor little slowpoke armadillo."

"Irene," warned Mama.

Robert opened his mouth to reply as his father spoke. "Irene, what happens on the hunt is men's business."

Irene was fit to be tied. She stuck her neck and chin out as far as it would go and fixed Robert with as threatening a glare as possible, her hands splayed on the table in front of her like a farmhand, and her elbows akimbo.

"Well, well, I bet you missed by a mile," she sputtered, too put out to talk straight. "It probably wasn't even fun!"

"It was too fun," was all Robert would concede. "Right, Daddy?"

"Sure was," he replied quickly. "Robert, first thing you take the wagon to the gin and pick up that baling wire. Now you both best get on with your chores, I've got to get goin' myself." He headed toward the back door.

"Daddy," called Irene.

"Not now, Irene, I'm late as it is. I mean it, time to get moving." Daddy was out the door and down the steps, Robert close behind him, before Irene could try again. Daddy gave Robert a wink as he headed off in the other direction.

Guess we did go huntin' after all, realized Robert with a smile. He took a deep breath and squared his shoulders like a man, heading off to do his chores.

Irene glared at Robert's back through the screen door.

"Shooting the evil eye at Robert is not going to change anything, young lady," Mama declared. "Get going on that laundry."

Irene grabbed the laundry basket and flounced out of the house. Another Saturday morning doing chores, she thought.

"Darn, darn, darn! I can shoot just as well as Robert and Homer. Better, even. And I sure can drive that wagon." Irene kicked the wicker basket along the ground under the clothesline and complained to the air while she threw the clothes over the line and jammed the clothespins onto them.

She could hear Robert bringing the wagon out of the barn and heading toward her along the yard road.

He tossed Irene a wave as he rolled by, looking for all the world like the king of the mountain.

Irene barely turned away from the clothes, waving vaguely in his direction. I bet he took some of his money for a soda at the gin store, too, she thought, giving the basket another kick. She peeked through the clothes and watched him drive away. Daddy was coming right toward her. Now was the time, she decided.

"Daddy!" she called.

"Hey there, Li'l Bit, helping your mama, are you?"

"Daddy, why can't I drive the wagon? You know I can drive it just as good as Robert. Look at my muscle." She flexed her arm in front of his face.

"Yes, sir, that's an impressive arm for a girl," he said, giving it a squeeze.

"See? Daddy, you're always telling me I'm a girl."

"Well, honey, you sure do look like a girl to me. And a mighty cute one at that."

"Daddy, it's not fair that girls don't get to go hunting or drive wagons. Mama drives sometimes. I want to go to the gin. It's just straight down our road and one left turn at Mr. Connors's fields. What if I didn't have any brothers? Why can't I, Daddy?"

He looked at Irene and sighed.

"Truth is, I never thought about it, Irene. It's always been a boy's job. Tell you what, I'll talk to your ma and we'll think on it." Giving her a pat, he walked away.

Well, at least that's something, she thought.

Irene was sitting on the pasture fence post when Daddy drove by in the wagon the next weekend.

"C'mon up and keep me company," he called.

Irene climbed up and Daddy handed her the reins.

"Why don't you take us over to the field yonder so I can check on the barbed wire along the back."

Irene was so tickled she didn't say a word. She sat straight up, gathered the reins, and set the wagon rolling. Irene was careful to stay in the hard-packed track. When they arrived at the back forty, Daddy made her stop, back up, turn around, and wait while he fussed with the fence. Finally, they headed home to the barn. The mules always picked up their pace going toward home, but she was careful to keep a tight hold on the reins so they didn't pull out of the track and head into the fields. Sneaking a look out of the corner of her eye, she could see Daddy was pleased. They came to a gentle halt in front of the barn.

"Hang on a minute while I put a few things in the back," he said. He dropped in some sacks and tools and came around front to look up at her.

"Why don't you drop off those sacks for me down at the gin for Mr. Connors and give those tools to the head man, then mosey on back here. They'll take them out of the wagon for you. Don't be dawdling too late, though. Remember dinner's at five." He gave Irene a wink and a smile as he stepped back.

"Daddy, can I truly?" Irene couldn't believe it. He really was letting her drive the wagon all by herself. She turned the wagon and headed on past Ring's favorite spot in the drive. She guided the mules around him and called, "Bye, Robert," to the figure bent over the dog. Robert was too shocked to answer. Irene thought she saw his mouth hanging open.

Irene couldn't see the gin yet past the bend at Mr. Connors's fields, but she could begin to smell the burning cotton husks. She guided the mules closer to the right and looked around at the half-harvested fields. When she rode along the road during cotton-growing season, it was like being above the clouds. This time of the year, near the end of the harvest, the fields always looked naked to Irene. But she had a chance to notice the other things alongside the road, like the paddle-shaped prickly pear cactus with their long spines glistening in the sun, and the squiggly mesquite trees along the boundaries of the fields. She had to be careful to keep the wheels off the edge so she didn't slide into the deep drainage ditches. It seemed impossible during the dry summers that they could fill up during the rainy season. Trying to relax her shoulders, Irene readjusted her hold on the reins. This sure beats hanging laundry, she thought, enjoying the pure pleasure of it all.

Irene loved the hustle and bustle of the gin, especially the pungent odor of the burning cotton husks mixed with machine oil. She listened carefully over the steady sound of the mules' hooves on the dirt road and the creaking of her wagon. She was barely able to hear the clanking of the machinery from here.

One day her teacher had taken the whole class over to see the gin. They'd all piled in her wagon for the short ride. Even though they'd studied the Industrial Revolution and Eli Whitney's invention, it was amazing to think someone had figured out a way to build it. She wondered if men really were smarter; they always seemed to be the ones doing the inventing.

It seemed no time at all before she arrived at the gin and pulled up to the large door.

"Well, I'll be danged," said one of the men standing around, "that's Henry's girl!"

"Don't that beat all, a girl coming to the gin!"

The foreman came out and reached into the back for the sacks.

"You men ought to know full well that if Henry let her drive to the gin, she sure knows what she's about."

Irene wanted to ask where the outhouse was, but

she didn't know where to tie the team and figured the men would just make fun of her.

"Please be sure to mark those sacks for Mr. Connors, and Daddy said the tools are for the head man," she called. "Thank you for unloading the wagon."

"My pleasure, Missy. You come back anytime. It sure is good to see a pretty face around here for a change."

Irene felt her face turn red as she bent down to pick up the reins and got ready to turn around. One of the men took the lead mule by the cheek strap and guided her back toward the gate.

"Next time I see your pa I'll tell him you did a real good job. Times sure are changing, I guess. With Mrs. Roosevelt in the White House, there'll be no stoppin' you gals. Now, you take care on your way back—sometimes these mules get it in their heads to have their dinner a mite too quick."

"Yes, sir," replied Irene. "Thank you." She gave the mules a slap on their rumps with the reins and headed on back toward home, feeling so proud she thought she'd bust. The wagon was lighter and the mules were flicking their ears toward home. There was a spring in their gait that Irene could understand.

A squeak of wheels behind made her turn and take a look. A dusty cloud was following another wagon, moving at a steady clip.

The other wagon pulled alongside, crowding her slightly.

"Well, Irene Hutto! You steal those mules? Where you going, to the glue factory? Ain't no one in their right mind going to give a good team of mules to a girl."

"James Tilley, shows how much you know! You're nothing but a nuisance," she replied coolly, without turning her head toward him.

James leaned his stringy body half off his seat and poked her team with his switch.

"Look, they're half dead," he said. "Mine could beat yours without half trying."

"They're the best mules in the county, and the fastest, when they want. You know mules don't pay any mind unless they're in the mood." Irene wished they would go a little faster. All this jiggling on the hard seat was making her think too much about having to use the outhouse.

"You couldn't make those mules run if your wagon was on fire," he taunted.

Irene stiffened her back. Ignore him, she told herself, it's only a couple of miles after I get around the bend.

"Of course, I forgot that you're such a baby. I heard you couldn't even get a little mouse out of your shirt without crying—you had to have your grandpa help you. The whole school knows."

"James Tilley, I bet there's something you wouldn't have down your shirt either. You're just trying to get me into trouble and I know it. Go away."

"Sissy girl," he sang out, giving his mules a swat and passing her at a trot. He wiggled his shoulder at her, batted his eyelashes, and brushed a hand delicately through his brown hair, pretending to primp. After a minute he dropped back alongside and started bumping her wheels with his.

"Bet I could push you right into the ditch and you'd be too scared to stop me," he said, sneering. "Girls shouldn't be allowed to do a man's job. Anyway, you're only strong enough to lift a laundry basket. 'Oh, James,'" he said in a high feminine voice, " 'you're scaring me. Go away.' "

He was just too much to tolerate, Irene decided.

She'd show him a thing or two about what a girl could do.

Irene slowly moved her feet wider apart against the foot brace and bent down as if she was going to fix her boot. She shortened the reins while she sat back up and got the mules' attention. Suddenly she leaned forward and slapped the reins on their rumps and let them slide loose through her fingers.

"Gee up!" she shouted.

Luckily the mules realized they were heading home and decided to run while given the chance. Irene was astounded at how quickly they could move; she didn't ever remember seeing mules take off this fast. Her arms were almost yanked right out of their sockets and she had to squint her eyes shut to keep out the dust. She didn't dare turn her head to see if James was coming; she didn't think she could move it, anyway. The fields were a blur on each side, and she decided maybe this wasn't such a good idea. If she came home with the team all sweaty, Daddy and Grandpa would know right away they'd been running.

She tried to rein them in, but just like mules, they

were going to get home their own way, fast. Oh my gosh, the bend's coming up, she realized. Leaning back with all her strength only seemed to make the team more determined. She could hear James yelling something behind her, but she couldn't make it out over the racket of her wheels. Maybe the wagon was going to come apart, she worried. Just let us get back in one piece, and I'll never do this again, prayed Irene.

Suddenly it seemed as though someone lifted her off the seat and gave her a gentle push through the air, like when she jumped off the rope at the creek. Slowly, dreamlike, she sailed over the ditch. Then she saw a flash of sunlight and blue, blue sky as she landed on her backside with a hard thump in a whirl of green. She could hear a crunch and splintering sound and felt suddenly heavy without the movement of the wagon under her. She could see the wagon wheels spinning wildly at a crazy angle just to her left and hear the mules snorting and hawing. It was hard to tell which way was up.

What's all this green around me? she wondered. Am I in heaven? In a daze, Irene tried to sit up. She knew, in an agonizing moment, where she was. A cactus patch! Then it started. Sharp, hot needles were sticking through her overalls and shirt. Her whole body was suddenly on fire. She looked up to see James staring down at her, horrified.

"Irene! Irene, say something," he begged. "I told you to watch the bend!"

Irene couldn't hear a thing but the loud wailing coming out of her mouth. It didn't even seem to be her own voice. She was afraid to move a muscle and thought surely she was going to burn up right then.

James reached into the prickly pear, grabbing Irene around the front of her overalls and one wrist. In a single motion he yanked her up and flung her over his shoulder. He crossed through the ditch and laid her on her stomach in his wagon.

"I'll take you home, don't you worry," he yelled. He quickly unhitched her mules and tied them to his wagon, then jumped in and tried to concentrate on getting to Irene's without too much bouncing or being distracted by her screaming.

They pulled up to the Homeplace and were quickly surrounded by her family. Irene didn't even care about her father's anger, she just wanted to stop the fire all over her body. Daddy and Grandpa Hutto lifted her quickly out of the wagon, feeling for broken bones as they laid her on her stomach on the couch.

"You're a lucky one, Irene, but you aren't going to think so for a while. Now, be brave while Mama gets these stickers out. You'll be all right, but when you're feeling better, we're going to have a talk about this," Daddy said.

Irene spent the rest of that day and most of the evening across her mother's lap, while Mama plucked all those cactus spines from her backside.

"I don't think you'll be wanting to be driving any wagon for a while," Mama remarked. "I don't know when you're going to learn to act like a lady."

Irene was glad no one else mentioned the mules or the wagon just then. Mama placed plasters on the wounds to draw out any infections and put her in bed, where she stayed for the better part of a week.

As she was lying there feeling sorry for herself one afternoon, in walked James Tilley.

"I'm sorry I teased you into racing, Irene," he said, his deep blue eyes serious. "I told your grandpa and father it was my fault. I even told that I bumped your wheels and was being ugly to you. And I told them how good you drove that wagon. You can ride with me anytime and I'll let you drive," he said earnestly.

Irene was still covered in bandages and her backside was lit on fire, but nothing that whole long week was as soothing or made her feel as good as hearing James Tilley apologize.

The Unexpected Voyage

"Ow, ow, ow! You're killing me, Aunt Belle!"

"Lucy, you're such a tender head!" Aunt Belle inched the brush through Lucy's curls.

"I wish I could just leave it all braided, even when I sleep. I hate it! Irene's is nice and straight."

"Just wait, Irene will want your hair when the boys start coming around. Joseph always says it was my hair that he noticed first, wanted to put flowers right in it, he said."

Lucy imagined standing on a bridge over the Seine River in Paris with a romantic Frenchman, her hair full of flowers and her own manuscript tucked under her arm.

She tried to button her nightgown again. "These buttons are so tiny, Aunt Belle. How can you do them?"

"It was the fashion in my grandma's day, Lucy. Sometimes they needed a buttonhook to pull them through the holes. This was her wedding nightgown, and she gave it to me when Joseph and I got married." Belle continued to brush Lucy's thick red hair gently as she spoke.

"I'm so worried I'll snag it. How ever can you let me wear it?" Lucy admired her reflection in the mirror over the dressing table.

"I think anyone who's going to grow up and be a writer in Paris ought to get used to fine things. When you're famous you can send me a French nightgown with lace all around the neck."

"Oui!" exclaimed Lucy, tickled. Between Belle and Lola, Belle was her favorite aunt. She never made fun of her plans to become a writer, and coming to help her with the chores while Joseph was gone was almost like a real vacation. The baby was due soon and Mama had sent her, not Irene, to take care of her own youngest sister. It was strange to sleep all by herself and she had to admit she missed Irene. But mostly only at night.

"I wonder what Irene's doing," she mumbled.

"Probably going to sleep, like you," said Belle. She went over to close the window against the rain. "This is a real windy one," she said, peering outside. As

Belle bent over to tuck her in, Lucy snuggled deeper into the feather mattress.

"This is so soft, Belle! It's like being in a cloud!"

"Good night, sweet dreams, angel!" said Belle as she closed the door from the bedroom into the front room. "See you in the morning!"

When I live in Paris, the first thing I'll buy is a nice soft bed like this, thought Lucy. She stretched out, spread-eagled. She could never do that at home, or Irene would poke her. It was so cozy to hear the rain drumming like pebbles on the window, listen to the wind, and to be so soft and warm. The gentle scent of flowers teased her nose every time she fluffed the sheet, but it was hard to concentrate on which ones they were, she was so sleepy.

Her aunt's voice seemed to be coming from far away. Was she calling her from the yard? Dimly Lucy heard the bedroom door burst open and saw the silhouette of her aunt's loose hair bend over her.

"Wake up, Lucy! The water's rising fast and we have to move the rugs and lift the furniture. Hurry! I need your help."

Lucy turned to the window as she jumped out of bed. The drumming now sounded like BB pellets, and she could see a tree bent almost all the way over out in the yard. It was hard to make out without much moonlight, but she thought she could see water beyond the porch rail.

"It's seeping in under the doors, come on!"

The rug had been partly rolled back against the couch, but there was a steady stream coming under the front door. Lucy knotted up her gown and grabbed the end of the couch.

"One-two-three-lift," said Belle. "No, wait! Help me get the things out of the bottom of the kitchen cupboards first. Hurry! We can dry out the rug."

They raced toward the back into the kitchen with the water after them like a slithering dark snake. She thought her aunt looked like an angel or a witch, depending upon the light.

I must look the same way, thought Lucy, putting her hand up to her head as she bent over the cupboard.

"The water hasn't come up this far as long as I can remember. I guess the bay's gone over the banks."

"I thought the bay was far away," said Lucy, straining to drop her armload on the counter.

"We're on low ground on this side near Taft, not like your Homeplace. I didn't think the storm would be this bad, though. Lordy, I bet this is a full-blown hurricane!"

A splintering and crunching sound brought them to attention. Looking through the doorway at the front door, they could see its bottom hinge had given way and water was pouring in around the door as if someone was pumping it.

"Oh!" cried Belle. "Hurry, we have to find something to hold on to if the door gives way. Something big enough for both of us, that'll float." They looked around frantically, their ankles in swirling water. The speed of the rushing water was frightening.

Just as the front door collapsed and lurched forward into the living room, they both focused on the back door with its large knob. The table would never get through the doorway.

"Lucy, help me get this loose," cried Belle, running to the door. "Get the poker over by the stove!"

Lucy couldn't move. The front doorway had become a charging wall of black water, at least as tall as herself. She wouldn't have been at all surprised to see a fire-breathing monster appear in the middle of it.

"Everything is lost," Belle said in a hushed tone. "Come on," she yelled as she grabbed Lucy around the waist with one arm and the doorknob with the other. "Hold on to the door and don't let go no matter what!" There was a deafening splintering noise and a sudden, powerful force of freezing water as it rushed over them. Lucy tried to catch a breath, and if Belle hadn't had such a tight grip on her, she never would have been able to remember to grab for the door. She couldn't believe what was happening, it was so quick, and sounded like a herd of longhorns at full tilt. As water crashed over them again, Lucy felt herself falling with the door as the whole backside of the house went down into the current.

The next thing she knew she was up to her neck in water, her aunt holding her fast and the door knocking her on the chin. It felt as if the water was grabbing her legs, twisting them out from under her, as if she would spin like a top if her aunt let go.

"Get up, get on, you can do it!" cried Belle. Lucy couldn't see a thing between the darkness and having to squeeze her eyes almost shut against the driving rain. She reached out toward her aunt's voice and struggled against the current to get a leg on board. She seemed to be sliding around like a greased pig, until a yank on her hair made her fly out of the water and land smack on top of Belle. Everything was so slippery she almost went right off the other side of the door, and she grabbed the only thing she could locate, winding her fingers and arms tightly into the thick wet mane of Belle's hair. Burying her head into Belle's neck, she could begin to catch her breath. Suddenly she realized they had lost their nightgowns, and their skin was black as the night. She felt sticky and slimy at the same time, and drilled by the rain as if it would leave permanent holes in her skin.

"Just hang on, Lucy, we'll land somewhere!" screamed Belle over the noise. It was hard to stay on Belle's back because she was lying sideways on account of the baby. Lucy hoped nothing would happen to the baby. She wondered what had happened to the animals in the barn and if chickens could swim. She'd just seen a frightened cow whirl by them, and a large branch. For a moment she thought she saw the huge oil refineries, but that was impossible; she knew they were on her side of the bay, not

Belle's. All the while the terrible rain drilled into them relentlessly.

She wound her fingers tighter into Belle's hair and bent her head deeper into Belle's neck. It wasn't so frightening from beneath the mass of heavy hair. Belle's hair smelled like the truck engine. And it was like taffy in her fingers. They were moving so fast and she was so cold and shivering scared, she could barely think. Every now and then something would scrape over her, making her burrow even deeper into that haven of hair, till it was wound so many times around her arms, and her legs over Belle's hips were so tight, that she didn't know herself what was hair and whose arm or leg was where. Lucy squeezed her burning eyes shut and prayed. She just knew they were going to die and she'd never see Irene and her family again.

As she lay in her bed, Irene listened to the drumming rain and thought how different it would be to sleep alone at night without Lucy's solid body next to hers. So what if Lucy was now old enough to go help Aunt Belle? Aunt Belle's is only another piece of our

160-acre farm, she thought, near Grandma Haskell's, it's not so far away. She stretched out and felt like she was sleeping in a wide field. Irene couldn't decide if it felt good or not. When it rained this hard she liked to feel Lucy's warmth. She guessed she'd miss Lucy telling her all the stories she was writing in her diary. Lucy was almost as good at telling stories as Grandpa Hutto. Irene was just floating off to sleep when Daddy came in and scooped her out of bed and stood her on the floor.

"Hurricane!" he said urgently. "Li'l Bit, hang on, we're going to the hay bundles!" He grabbed her blanket, took her small hand in his, and began to pull her through the house. Still half asleep, Irene thought it was kind of dumb to go to a hay pile in a hurricane. Why not stay in a nice wooden house? Suddenly they were outside in the stinging rain and strong wind, and Mama was trying to gather all the shivering children around her.

"Irene," said Daddy, putting the baby in her arms, "you're strong enough to carry Baby Annie. When I say go, we'll run over and push straight through into the center of the bundle stack."

"But Daddy—"

"No time for arguments, you just do it. As soon as the eye hits, it'll be calm enough to move."

Homer looked at Irene.

"Into *dried-up bundles* in a hurricane?" he asked.

Irene shrugged, equally afraid.

There was a loud crack behind them. Who would be shooting a shotgun in the middle of a hurricane? wondered Irene, as everyone jumped. It was followed by a drawn-out splintering, then a whooshing sound and a thud, as the kitchen roof blew over their heads and landed smack in front of them, hurling toward the fields like a rolling ball. The family looked to Daddy for help.

"The hay bundles," he said. "We'll be safer there. The wind blows right through the bundle centers, but the pile is so thick it'll be safe underneath." Suddenly the wind and rain stopped, as if someone had turned a switch.

"Now!" shouted Daddy, pulling everyone behind him. They ran across the yard toward the side of the storage barn, and burrowed into the stack, Daddy struggling and pushing aside the scratchy bundles on the bottom layer to make a path. Irene and Annie huddled in the center with the rest of the family. As the wind howled, Irene prayed that the top bundles, all stacked like bricks to form a roof, would hold.

If the roof did come off, thought Irene, it would be just like the three little pigs' straw house. She squeezed her eyes shut, shivering under her wet blanket, and waited for the wolf to blow the house down.

It had seemed to take forever to stop. Irene couldn't remember so much rain at once. And the wind! Some of the bundles had escaped, but the haystack was better off than the rest of the yard, which was ankle deep in muddy water. Trees were broken and tossed all over, and a piece of the barn was over against a hole it had made in the bunkhouse. Luckily Thomas and Charley were okay. She hadn't liked when Charley moved out to the bunkhouse. She always felt safer when he was in the boys' room, especially when Mama and Daddy were away late.

Ring was running all around the outside of the henhouse, making those poor chickens even more crazy. The pigs were the only ones she could see who thought this was a perfect day.

Later in the morning she overheard her parents

talking softly, and thought she heard "low ground," but she wasn't sure. She was about to ask when Mr. Geary, a neighbor, pulled up to the back porch in his wagon and asked her father to come help search for missing people.

"What a mess everywhere," he said to her parents. "You'd hardly recognize anything. The oil refineries busted up and put slick on everything, and the bay came way over the banks. It's under water to the tops of houses over by Taft near your one-sixty, and we need all the hands we can get over here on our side by the refineries. You're lucky, most people over here had their houses come down on them and lost most their crops. Can you hitch up your wagon? Road's too wet for the trucks. They're digging mass graves to get ready. Not good to wait in the heat, you know."

"Our Lucy is with Belle over there by Taft, John," said Daddy. "We were just saying we had better go pick her up and see what's happened there. Joseph's away."

"Well, Henry, I'm truly sorry. I hope she's okay, but the bridge is out and the water's too high. There's no way over yet. Sure would appreciate it if you'd come help us. Seems we've got half of Taft floated over here."

"Well, I can't refuse, for sure. Mae, honey," he said to Mama, "now don't you worry, you know I'll get over there as soon as it's possible, even if we have to swim the mules. Charley, Homer, go hitch 'em up, y'all are big enough to come. Put in all the shovels we got, and some rope and blankets. Fill up some of the milk cans with fresh water, too."

Irene realized what her parents had been talking about. Lucy was on low ground near Taft, with Belle. She felt sick to her stomach. What if something bad had happened? Mr. Geary had said it was all under water up to the rooftops, and they couldn't even get over there to find her. So many people were missing or dead they needed Daddy's wagon, too.

Her mother's voice interrupted her thoughts.

"Irene, you bring in the children and we'll start our own dirty work."

Irene hesitated. Then she walked up to Daddy and looked him in the eye.

"I'm coming, too, Daddy," she said firmly. "Lucy's going to need me and I'm not going to sit here with all the little ones when I can help find her."

Daddy looked at Mama over Irene's head. He paused a moment before he said, "It's going to be pretty bad, Irene, but you're right. Get into your overalls and boots and we'll be going."

Irene followed Mama and the children into the kitchen and stared up at the blue sky.

"Good thing we went into the bundles!" said Robert.

Irene went to get dressed, her legs shaky.

"Well," said Mama, "we're all safe here and the rain's stopped. We're going to be a lot better off than some others. Doesn't do any good to fret about Lucy and Belle; you know Daddy will go there as soon as anybody can. There's nothing we can do except pray and take care of our own mess here."

It was slow going in the wagon as Daddy steered the mules among the debris left by the receding water.

"Gosh," exclaimed Irene. "Why's everything so black?"

"It's the oil, remember?" replied Charley.

"Look at all the animals over there," said Homer, pointing, "they're covered!"

In every direction along the flat countryside the scene was the same: bodies in grotesque positions, both animal and human. Trucks and wagons every which way, chickens, mules, and cows standing stock-still, looking like black rocks with dazed eyes. Everything was still. It seemed especially quiet after the noise of the storm. The baking sun was beginning to heat up the mud. Irene could smell the oil and some other bad odor that was a little like day-old pig slop.

Irene could still hear the storm in her head. It got louder all day as they picked up bodies and delivered them to the large graves. She saw grown men weep. Several times everyone was sick, Daddy too. Irene fought back tears when she thought of Lucy. She couldn't bring herself to ask Daddy what he thought; she knew they were all thinking it wasn't possible for her and Belle to have survived on low ground when this much damage had been done to their high side of the bay. Even though a lot of the floodwater had flowed into the drainage ditches, they were still up to their ankles in sticky black mud. Sometimes they had to get out and push the wagon.

"What's all the commotion?" Charley pulled up the

mules as Daddy climbed down into a group of men standing near a chicken coop. Irene was constantly amazed by what was left standing, due only to the whim of the water and the wind.

"Don't know for sure," replied a man nearest to him. "Seems there's a woman in there with the chickens, lost her clothes in the storm and she won't come out."

"Why, most people ended up the same way. What's so different about her?" asked Daddy.

"I've got enough problems, you can find out for yourself," said the man as he left.

Irene could hardly hear with all the squawking coming from the coop and the men yelling to the woman. They were throwing blankets in the door, but it apparently had no effect, she just didn't want to come out. Homer said he thought he heard crying, too, but it was hard to say, since by now it was just as noisy from the men getting tired of all the fuss.

"Think we haven't seen a naked lady, you there? Everybody lost their clothes! Now you grab those blankets and come on out. We got a lot to do without fussing here any longer!"

Daddy leaned toward the coop. Chickens were

coming out as if they'd been pushed, unable to flap their sticky wings.

"Here," said Daddy, as Irene, Homer, and Charley watched from the wagon. "Let me try, I've got a lot of women at home and they're tough critters when they want to be. Hush up and let me at it." Daddy took a blanket and walked close to the coop door.

"Now honey," he called gently. "Never you mind these men, they're just trying to get you some help. Lots of folks lost their clothes, and most a lot worse. Why don't you just grab one of these blankets and come on out. It can't be all that bad. Besides, we got to be getting on, so how about helping us out here?"

Irene jumped down next to Daddy and yelled out, "I can bring you a blanket if you want me to—I'm a girl, too." She ran over to Daddy, grabbed the blanket, and held it in her outstretched arm in front of the door, staying out of sight.

No answer. The men stayed quiet, expecting the squawking and screaming to start back up. Then they saw what looked like a chicken poke out of the door, but it was high up and moved like a hand. It moved down and snatched the blanket from Irene and yanked it back inside. She quickly ran to get another blanket and the same thing happened. Arms covered with feathers. Oil and feathers.

All of a sudden, two chickens wrapped in blankets and as tall as people came out of the door. You could barely see eyeballs. It took a moment for everyone to realize these were people, they had so much oil in their hair and over their bodies. It looked like a hawk had built nests on their heads. On top of the sticky oil were all the feathers it's possible to find in one chicken coop. One was taller and fatter than the other, but that's about all it was possible to tell. Irene was transfixed. She'd heard of being tarred and feathered in the old days, but never in a hundred years did she think she'd actually see it. Irene backed up next to Daddy.

"Lordy," said Daddy, smothering a smile. "Y'all sure do look a mess. Everything's going to be all right, don't you worry."

The small chicken-person took a tentative step forward.

"Daddy?" it said with Lucy's voice.

Sydney

"Thatta boy, Sydney," cooed Irene, reaching down to pat the muscular neck of the ex-racehorse. She wound her fingers in his snowy white mane and let her legs relax. Each morning she enjoyed the ride to school even more than the day before. Ever since Mama had begun letting her ride Sydney, she almost didn't mind anything that happened during the rest of the day. It was heaven to have a whole half hour of peace once she climbed on his warm bare back.

"Daddy will calm down," she said to Sydney. "Just you remember to behave now and we won't have any more trouble." Irene looked around as the horse followed Lucy and Lottie Mae on the pinto. Tall Lucy in front of stocky Lottie Mae exaggerated the plump pony's swaying back. It wasn't possible to see Robert and Homer on Sugar up ahead unless she leaned to the side, but Irene couldn't have been less interested anyway. Sometimes Irene got behind them just to watch Homer's jug ears sticking out above his skinny neck.

Now that she was out of sight of the farm, Irene lifted her feet up and undid her shoes, tying the laces together and draping them over Sydney's withers. I'm never going to outgrow these horrible things, she thought. And Lucy didn't have to wear them later since her feet were already bigger than Irene's. She was glad Sydney didn't mind them bouncing on his back. Irene didn't think it would be the same to ride with those heavy things stuck on her feet any more than she could imagine keeping them on all day in school.

"Irene," hollered Lucy, "what's keeping you?"

"Can't hear you," yelled Irene in return. No one, absolutely no one, was going to have any of her half hour with Sydney. Everything looks different from up here, she thought. I wonder if it's true that everything looks gray to horses. She could see almost all the way across Mr. Connors's freshly plowed fields on either side of her, even how deep the rows were, and how the black earth seemed lighter along the tops. She was glad Sydney liked to take his time on the way to school, but when Sydney galloped it was like a storm wind, only softer. It was amazing how she could feel him stretch his powerful legs so far. The faster he went, the smoother it got, until it was like rolling thunder under her. It sure was tempting to let him get started, even if it was a little scary.

"Good boy, Sydney," she said. "I like to run, too, but you know what Daddy said. I'm counting on you, boy. When Daddy's not so nervous, maybe he'll let us go for a gallop. Is that where Mama takes you, boy, huh? Look, there's the postman with the mail, re-member him? Hi, Mr. Battleman," she called with a wave. "He sure looks short, doesn't he?" she whis-pered.

"Hey, Irene! I see your mama must think you're kinda special to let you near her horse. Never thought I'd see the day he'd be poking along to school." He moved around to the back of his truck and pulled out some mail for the group of wooden boxes. "You take care now, Irene," he called.

"Irene, hurry up," yelled Robert. "We still got a mile to go."

"Can't hear you," she yelled back.

"It's almost true," she said to Sydney. "Stop twitch-ing your ears toward Mr. Battleman, they're already past the corner, see?" Irene leaned down next to Sydney's eye and pointed diagonally across the field to her left.

She tilted her head back and took a deep breath. The fall air was still balmy and the sun was warm on her face. "We could ride all the way to the Rockies, Sydney. Wouldn't you like to see snow? All we'd be able to see of you would be your black specks. I'll bet you'd like it, too. I wonder what it feels like?" Irene heard the mail truck passing them and picked up the halter lead to guide Sydney closer to the side of the road. She felt him tense his muscles as the truck passed by.

"No, Sydney!" she cried.

It was too late. She barely had time to lay flat against his neck and grab his mane with both hands, gripping his running body for dear life with her knees. She knew better than to waste her strength trying to stop him. He couldn't stand for anything to pass him—it didn't even matter which direction it was going. The mailman went straight on and turned left at the corner, Sydney in hot pursuit. She caught a glimpse of her brothers and sisters near him out of the corner of her eye. Suddenly the galloping horse took it into his mind to take the inside turn, as he must have been taught.

"No, not here!" yelled Irene. She almost slid off as Sydney lurched through the corner of the deeply furrowed soft dirt and then regained speed. In spite of her fear and the certainty that this was going to lead to disaster, Irene loved the feeling of his powerful body plunging through the field and filling her face with wind. Unfortunately Irene could also see Mr. Connors behind his plow off to the other side, and they seemed to be heading dangerously close.

"C'mon, Sydney," she gasped, her strength almost gone. "You've won, you've won!" The mail truck was out of sight and the others had stopped to watch. She could sense Sydney trying to make a decision about which way to go, and he seemed to be slowing down. Straight toward the farmer he went, a final burst of speed for the finish. Just past the plow Sydney came to an abrupt halt, sending Irene arching over his head like a stone from a slingshot.

Irene lifted her face and spit out a mouthful of dirt, raising herself off her stomach onto her elbows, trying to get her breath back. I can move everything, she thought, with a test of each limb. At least there's no cactus.

"Missy, you all right? You got no business on a horse goes that fast." The farmer was leaning over her, a worried look on his face.

"I'm okay, Mr. Connors, really. And he doesn't always go that fast, only when something passes him." She glanced over toward Sydney, now standing innocently next to the plow mule. He couldn't seem to understand what Irene was doing on the ground.

Irene got up slowly and brushed off as much of the sticky black earth as possible.

"I'm truly sorry he ruined your plowing, really I am," she said.

"The important thing is you're not hurt, Missy. I ought to have a word with your father about that horse, I should."

Irene hurried over to Sydney and picked up the halter lead.

"I'll tell him. No need for you to bother," she said. Quickly Irene led the horse over to the tree stump by her waiting brothers and sisters and climbed back on Sydney. The farmer followed her over and held the halter. "You sure you'll tell your pa what happened?" he insisted.

Homer volunteered quickly, "We sure will, Mr. Connors, but we got to be going to school. I'll come help you fix your field if you need."

"That's all right, you go on now. And you mind that horse, young lady! The county race is where he belongs."

The children hurried their horses along the road toward school.

"Now you've gone and done it, Irene. Daddy's going to sell him to the glue factory for sure."

"Homer Hardy, you hush up," scolded Lucy. "Irene's got enough to answer to when she gets home without you being a bother, too. Just once, leave her be. Are you all right?" she asked her sister. "You sure are dirty, even for you."

"Except for Daddy going to give Sydney away if he ran again," replied Irene. "And I had to go and fall off, too." She was beginning to feel all her bruises with each of Sydney's steps.

"Irene, you know that's Mama's horse and Daddy can't really say." Robert looked at her dirt covered head. "Boy! Bet we could plant some cotton right in your hair!"

"Where's your shoes?" Lottie Mae stared at Irene's blackened feet.

Irene looked down at Sydney's withers. "Guess they must be buried somewhere in the field." She looked at Lucy and grinned.

"Explain that one to Mama, Irene Frances Hutto."

"Homer, I've had enough out of you," said Irene, cutting him off as his voice squeaked out of control. "I'll think of something. And y'all know Mama always does what Daddy thinks best."

The ride home from school was solemn, each trying to think of a way to influence their father's decision. Irene was feeling terrible imagining being without Sydney. But it sure did seem that Mama had some mysterious connection with the horse that Daddy had no say over. Sometimes Irene heard Mama whispering and laughing to her parents about Sydney.

Irene tried to slip in the kitchen door behind the others, but it was no use.

"Irene! How'd you get so dirty? I declare, you look

like something the cat drug in. And where are your shoes?" Mama came over and turned Irene all around and waited for an answer.

"I tripped in the school yard and then two more kids stumbled over me and we all got mixed up," explained Irene. "And I took off my shoes after 'cause I got dirt inside them and then I set them on the steps while I went to get Sydney and when I came back they weren't there," said Irene all in one breath. "I think that mean James Tilley hid them on me."

"I think that gawky James is sweet on Irene," piped in Homer, with a sharp jab of his bony elbow into her ribs.

"He is not!" cried Irene indignantly.

Robert gave her a poke, too.

"That's what I hear," he said, trying to deliver a look to Irene that said shut up.

"Now you children leave Irene alone," Mama said. "And you go clean up down by the pump, Missy. I don't know how a girl could get so dirty. Leave those clothes out on the porch."

"C'mon, I'll help you," said Lucy, yanking Irene out the door before she could put her bare foot any farther into her mouth.

At dinner that evening their father was sitting stiffly at the table, their mother fussing over by the stove.

"Saw Mr. Connors this afternoon over by the gin, Irene," he said quietly. "Anything you got to tell me?"

All the children fell silent. Irene swallowed several times before any words would come out of her mouth.

"It wasn't Sydney's fault, Daddy. The mail truck scared him and I just slid off."

"Irene, you know nothing scares that horse except being left behind. He'd chase his own tail if it got in front of him. I told you if this happened again he'd have to be sold. We can't afford to have an animal that doesn't earn its keep, even with the government offering to buy our surplus crops, thanks be to President Roosevelt. You were just plain lucky not to get hurt, not to mention making more work for Mr. Connors. And all of you," he said, looking around the table, "haven't told the truth. We can't abide any of this."

"Please, Daddy, I can think of something. We can't sell Sydney, he's been part of the family since any of us can remember. Pretty soon he'll be too old to run."

"Henry," said Mama, "maybe we ought to give Irene a chance. After all, it is Sydney, Henry, remember?" She smiled at her husband ever so slightly as she sat down.

"Hmmmm," he replied, giving Mama a steady look. "Well then, no more riding that horse until we figure out a solution. Irene, it's up to you. We've tried everything we could think of. After a few days, we'll decide what to do. Now eat your dinner, everyone, we've spent enough talk on that racehorse."

"We'll see," said Mama softly, lifting her fork. "Homer, quit stuffing your mouth and chew your food like a gentleman or you'll eat in the pantry."

The next morning Irene went out to her special thinking place in the barn.

"I wish Grandpa wasn't busy," she said to the heifer. "He always knows what to do, don't you think so?" E.B. regarded her solemnly. "I swear you look like you're ready to talk. If there really is that reincarnation thing, then right now is the time to do it." She gave the cow a hard look. "Well, you never did come up with any good ideas," she said. "You're probably enjoying this." She went outside and started off toward the chickens, glancing at the grain silo. She still shuddered when she thought of that mushy mouse down her shirt.

Remembering E.B. pestering everyone, she continued to mumble to herself. "You always cheated, too, had to peek so you'd win. We should've fixed you with a blindfold." Still, she missed those times when E.B. wasn't obnoxious.

Irene went into the henhouse to get the feed bucket. She came outside and covered her eyes from the bright sun with one hand.

"Now, where is that darn rooster?" she said aloud. She opened her fingers slightly and turned around at a sound behind her. "Ha! I see you! Don't think you can hide behind me and eat everyone's breakfast! Shoo, go on!" She chased the brazen bird off to the side and reached into the bucket for grain to fling toward the hens. Irene finished her chore and headed toward the outhouse.

Irene hated the outhouse, but Mama and Papa said they couldn't afford one of those inside toilets yet, just the kitchen cold-water spigot from the tank. Sometimes it wasn't bad, you could read the old

Sears catalogs left in there. She put her hand over her nose to take a breath. Even the lime Daddy threw in never helped much. She moved the catalog to keep it in the strip of sunlight falling through the wall cracks onto her lap. She hated it when the boys used the pages with pretty clothes first and left the ones with the dumb tools. Her eye was caught by the picture of a horse head. "Does your horse spook easily?" read the caption. "Attach a pair of our leather blinders and your problems will be solved." I never heard of a blindfold for a horse, she thought. How do they see where they're going? She read the rest of the information. "Cut out all distracting objects from your horse's side vision. Guaranteed to keep his eyes on the road ahead." Irene almost shouted to her father right then. She was so excited she almost wiggled her behind, remembering her last splinter just in time. She thought about putting her hand over her eyes just a minute ago. It really works, she realized. I couldn't see the rooster, and we used to see E.B. cheat in hide 'n seek because he had to turn his head to peek through his fingers.

After ripping out the page and using another, Irene quickly yanked up her overalls. She burst out of the door into the fresh air and ran to find her father.

She rushed up to Sydney near the corral fence. "Don't worry, Sydney, I figured it out! You won't have to leave and I can still ride you to school, and we can make them ourselves and stick them on your halter. See?" She waved the picture in front of the startled horse and gave him a tight hug around his neck and a kiss on his cheek.

Irene ran off toward the nearby field. "Daddy, Daddy," she called, "I found it, I found it, I know how to fix Sydney!"

"Hang on there a minute, Li'l Bit, I got to finish this row." A few moments later Daddy came over to her and said, "What's all this noise about, now? You keep wiggling like that and you'll drill yourself right into the ground."

Irene showed Daddy the page. "See, Daddy, they're just squares of leather nailed onto the outsides of his cheek straps, and we have lots of old harness. We could put them together and then Sydney couldn't see anything passing him. He doesn't care if someone's already in front. Please, Daddy, can't we try them?"

Daddy read the description and studied the picture. A smile spread over his face, and he gave Irene a squeeze.

"You just might have done it, honey. Don't see why we can't give it a try. Aren't you sharp as a tack to have figured this out! And all by yourself, too. Why don't you run show Mama this and tell her we'll make some soon as we can."

Irene had never known her father to agree to something so quickly.

"I knew you loved Sydney, too, Daddy," said Irene. She was pretty sure her father had let out a sigh of relief when he read that page. She galloped off through the dirt yard, scuffling toward the vegetable garden, one hand alongside each eye.

Mama was sitting at the garden table shelling peas. When Irene told her about the blinders, she was as excited as Irene.

"I'm real proud of you, Irene. All this time and no one ever thought of blinders. Isn't that a wonder! I'll bet your daddy was mighty pleased, too," she hinted.

"How'd you get a racehorse anyway, Mama?"

Mama smiled and took Irene's hand, leading her over to the bench.

"I guess if you and I are going to share Sydney,

then you're old enough to know why he's so special," she said. "It'll be just between you and me and Daddy. Daddy can't give Sydney away," she began mysteriously. "That's why he was so happy to have you come up with a solution to his dilemma.

"My father bought Sydney from a horse trainer and gave him to me. One day when I was about seventeen your daddy saw our family pass by in our wagon on the way to church. He said later that right then he decided he was going to marry me. We started court- ing, though you can imagine I wasn't all that inter- ested in getting married just then, even though my parents were real anxious that I was getting on in age. So I told Daddy I'd never marry anybody unless they'd take Sydney, too. You can understand why I didn't want to give up Sydney, can't you?" she asked.

Irene thought of the way she felt so free on his back, especially when he galloped. She nodded her head, not wanting to interrupt the story.

"And nobody had any money to spare then. Even so, Daddy came over to the farm when I was busy with my chores and my father sold him that horse just as quick as could be, once Daddy told him what I'd said. At first I was real mad, because Daddy plain gave me no choice. He knew I meant what I'd said about Sydney. Then I realized that any man who'd promise to keep my horse no matter what had to be as kind and generous as I thought he was. And sure enough, I made up my own mind real quick when I figured that out. You're right about Sydney being a member of the family." Mama laughed.

Irene was fascinated. Her daddy acting so crazy? Just like some prince in a fairy tale. And she had to admire his trick. She looked at Mama, smiling over her memory of the bargain and enjoying Daddy's predicament this week. I guess Mama really does like to make up her own mind, she thought. Just like me. She grinned back at Mama and they laughed together.

"Don't you dare tell your daddy I told you yet," said Mama. "Sometimes men feel like they need to make all the decisions."

"Don't worry, Mama, I won't tell nobody. I sure am glad you told me, though. And my shoes, Mama, I think they're out there somewhere in Mr. Connors's field," she blurted.

Mama smiled at Irene. "I figure they're plowed under by now, honey, don't you? We'll go find your next pair, instead of Daddy. I think you're old enough not to wear someone's old brass-toe work boots."

Irene gave her a mother a hug and rested her head on Mama's shoulder for a moment.

"I love you, Mama," she said quietly. "I guess I better go do my chores."

"Give Sydney a kiss for me on your way to the barn, honey."

Irene put her hands back up alongside her eyes and galloped off.

The Visit

"Mama, I promise! If you let me stay with Grandma and Grandpa, I'll be good as gold." Irene clutched her mother's hand as she pleaded.

"Sugar, I know you would be. But you're such a help at home that I don't know if we can do without you for two weeks."

"Mae, Irene's going to grow up sooner or later. She deserves to have her own time with us. Heck, I deserve a chance to have this grandbaby alone." Grandma Haskell put her arm around Irene's narrow shoulders. "It's only two weeks, not forever. There's plenty of clothes around here for her to wear."

Irene watched her mother consider. The other children were squabbling in the wagon over who would sit where. Please, thought Irene, let me stay. She knew she would be expected to pitch in for chores, but at least there wouldn't be any baby-sitting here.

"No fuss, you'll help your grandparents?"

"Cross my heart and hope to die," squealed Irene, wiggling back and forth with excitement.

"Good, now that's settled," said Grandma quickly. "Mae, climb up in that wagon so y'all get home before dark. I thought you learned to drive that fancy new Ford truck."

"I still prefer the horses or the mules, Mama. They're easier on these dirt roads. Maybe when they finish putting down the macadam. Now, you behave, Missy, and enjoy your vacation." Mama gave Irene a hug.

Irene and Grandma watched Homer drive slowly down the road, his bony shoulders squared proudly.

"Good-bye!" shouted everyone. Little Edward waved so hard only Lucy's quick grab saved him from tumbling off the back of the wagon.

"Lordy," said Grandma, "we'd better step inside before someone gets hurt. Know what we're going to do? We're going to get our chores out of the way so you and I can take on old sol and beat him."

Grandma must know at least a hundred ways to play solitaire, thought Irene. "Should I feed the chickens?" she asked.

"Fine and dandy," replied Grandma. "Run on down to the barn and collect the feed pail, fill it about three quarters full, and when you're in the pen make sure that banty rooster doesn't make a pig of himself." Grandma fished a rag out of her apron and gave it to Irene. "Wave this dishrag at him if he gets too uppity."

Irene threw feed at the chickens from the middle of the pen, occasionally looking over at Grandpa filling the pigpen trough. "Git," she said to the banty, waving the rag. I'll have to try a rag at home, she thought, it really works.

Irene saw Grandpa shield his eyes and peer into the distance. She finished her job and joined him, squinting to cut the glare. There seemed to be someone walking.

"Are we expecting visitors?" she asked.

"Nope. It's mighty darn warm to be trudging around the countryside. Don't usually have people walk in."

"Grandpa, it looks like two people, a child and a lady. She's carrying something."

"Guess I'll mosey on down and see if I can help

out. Coming?" Grandpa knew Irene's curiosity was itching.

The woman attempted to wave her hand but it was burdened with a packet. Her other arm clutched a baby. A small dusty boy straggled behind her, carrot-red hair stuck to his sweaty forehead.

"I'll be danged . . . Lurleen Davis! What the heck brings you way out here?"

"Mr. Haskell, I'm . . ." As she turned to wait for the boy, tears spilled down her cheeks. "I'm . . . I didn't know where else to come."

"Honey, take it easy." Grandpa took the packet, bent down, and lifted the little boy. "Let's go on up to the house and get y'all something to drink. Irene, why don't you run ahead and tell Grandma we're coming."

Who were these people? The woman had a black eye, and when Grandpa lifted the package Irene had seen an ugly bruise covering her forearm, like when the mule kicked Charley in the thigh. She bolted through the kitchen door.

"Grandma! Grandma! We got visitors and I think the lady got herself kicked by a mule! She's crying."

"What are you talking about, child? Who's coming?"

"Grandpa called her Doreen or Darlene or something."

Grandma wiped her hands on her apron as she stood at the back door watching the small group approach.

"I declare, that's Lurleen. My goodness, haven't seen her since she ran off with that Davis boy." Grandma stepped into the yard.

"Lurleen, welcome to our home. Look at you, all dusty." Nervously Grandma glanced over her shoulder at Irene in the doorway. "Come on in and get a cool drink, we'll talk later. Here, let me take that baby off your hands."

"I think Lurleen and her little ones are going to rest with us a spell," Grandpa said. "Irene, maybe you could fetch some quilts and make up a pallet in your room for these babies."

"That's a good idea," said Grandma. "Lurleen, what are these children's names?"

"This here is Jimmy and the baby's June."

"Irene, could you take Jimmy and clean him up a

bit? Probably cool him right down to have a bath, then he could help you with that pallet."

So much for not watching anybody, thought Irene, but she saw she didn't have a choice; the little boy's sweaty body was covered in dust.

"Jimmy, how about we go out by the well and fill the tub? Uncle Jack made a boat to play with and you can sail it."

The old galvanized tub filled quickly with both Irene and Jimmy working the pump handle.

"Jimmy, how old are you? Six?" His eyes leaped to Irene's face.

"Nope."

"Seven?"

"Nope, four and a half!"

"Four and a half! You could have fooled me. I have a little brother about your age. You're much bigger. Are you sure you're only four and a half?" Jimmy nodded and smiled while Irene unbuttoned his shirt. "Okay. Can you finish undressing and get in or do you need a boost?"

"I can do it. I'm a big boy. I'm Mama's little man. I can do most everything by myself. I'm not even afraid to put my head in the water. Wanna see?" He jumped in and disappeared underwater before Irene could reply.

Irene put the small wooden boat in the water and handed him Grandma's homemade soap. "What happened to your mama? Did she get kicked by a mule?"

"Mule? We don't have no mule."

"Did she have an accident? She has a black eye."

Jimmy became very still. After a moment he stood up. "I'm finished now. I want to go inside." Irene noticed his lip quiver, and hugged him into a towel. She'd have to ask Grandma what kind of an accident later.

Approaching the screen door, Irene heard Grandma speaking softly.

"Honey, no one should have to put up with this kind of treatment. You didn't do—" She broke off as the door opened.

"Well, here they are. And don't you look good enough to snuggle, Jimmy. Come on over here and let's get a look at you."

Grandpa gave Irene a pat on the back. "Thanks, honey."

"Grandma, I didn't know what to put on him."

"There's a flour sack in the back bedroom closet and a few extra things in there. Why don't you and Jimmy go see what you can find?"

"That's okay," said Lurleen. "He's got a change in the bundle. Thanks, Irene."

During dinner Grandma chattered like a magpie. Irene was glad; it gave her time to watch the mysterious and sad Lurleen. The black eye was nearly matched by the dark circles under her eyes, and the bruises on her forearm looked like purple stripes. Maybe someone had grabbed her. Something bad must have happened to take away an appetite for Grandma's cooking. Lurleen hadn't done anything but push her food around.

"Everybody get enough to eat? Good," continued Grandpa quickly. "Irene, would you do Lurleen a favor and get these babies down? I think she could use a breather."

"Sam, I'll do it," said Grandma. "Irene could use one, too."

"I'll do it, Mrs. Haskell. You've done plenty already and they'll go down better if it's me." She lifted June out of the chair, taking Jimmy by the hand. "Come on, Jimmy, I'll tell you a story," she said as they left the room.

Helping Grandma wash up, Irene blurted, "Grandma, who is Lurleen? Is she family? She looks sad. What happened to her and why does she have those bruises?"

"Missy, you sure ask a lot of questions, not all of them polite. Lurleen isn't exactly family. She was close friends with your aunt Belle growing up. Used to see a lot of her then."

"But what about her bruises?"

Grandma busied herself in the pantry. "Like I said, not all your questions are polite. If she wants to tell you, she will. Otherwise, don't ask."

"Well, I just thought maybe she had an accident."

Weary, Grandma sighed. "You'll understand more when you're older, Irene." Then she smiled. "You want to take on a couple of games of ol' sol before bedtime?"

"Can you teach me pyramid solitaire again? I keep forgetting how it goes."

"Sure, go get the cards and we'll play here at the table."

Snuggled in bed later with the children sleeping quietly on the pallets, Irene strained to hear the adults' conversation in the sitting room.

"You're welcome here as long as you need to stay," said Grandpa.

"I just need a couple of days to let T.J. simmer down—he always does. It was my fault. He can't stand to have anything out of place, and I left that seed catalog on the floor by the bed."

Grandma murmured, "Lurleen, honey, a man shouldn't grab you so tight he leaves a bruise like that. It's just plain mean."

Irene pulled the sheet tight up to her chin. Her stomach hurt. It wasn't an accident, she realized. Lurleen's husband made those bruises. No wonder Grandma didn't want her to ask questions. What was so bad about leaving a seed catalog on the floor?

"T.J. needs to control that famous temper of his. I think someone needs to talk to him," said Grandpa.

Good, thought Irene, he'd have to listen to Grandpa.

"Oh no, Mr. Haskell, don't! He'd just get mad,"

said Lurleen. She sounded scared. "Being without work is hard on a man, it's made him more short-tempered."

"Plenty of men out of work right now, Lurleen. Lots of men having problems with this Depression. It doesn't excuse his taking it out on you." Grandpa sighed.

"It'll be a quiet chat, Lurleen. I can't let you go back to him without saying anything."

Irene wondered what her grandpa was going to say.

The sitting room grew quiet but Irene lay awake. Why would anyone hurt someone they loved because of something so dumb? Sometimes Mama and Daddy got angry with each other and it scared Irene to hear them raise their voices, but this didn't seem the same. Mr. Davis should have just yelled if he was so mad.

A short while later the door opened and Irene felt Lurleen crawl into the other side of the bed. She wished she could reach out and pat Lurleen's back, but she stayed as quiet and still as she could.

In the morning Irene slipped out of bed. Approaching the kitchen door, she paused when she heard her grandparents' low voices.

"Sam, that boy has always been trouble. You're going to stir him up and make it worse for her."

"Somebody has to let him know he can't keep on like this. I want him to understand I'll be listening for any rumor he's knocking her around."

"What if he comes after you?"

"His kind of man never gets in a fight with someone who can actually give him a run for his money."

"I wish she'd leave him, go home and live with her parents."

"Her folks think she made her own bed and they'd send her back, even if they aren't crazy about him. It's just not done, leaving your husband."

"Lordy, sometimes life sure is hard. Couldn't we let her stay with us, Sam? It does get lonesome here without all the children."

"Sugar, we can offer but I don't think she's ready to take us up on it."

There was a pause and Irene started to move. She stopped again when she heard Grandpa say, "Guess I better get going. I'll stop in at the Harveys' and use their telephone. I'll have my chat with that boy and tell him he can come around tomorrow. You need anything from town?"

"Why don't you see if Mr. Gladstone's got any of those peppermint sticks Irene likes. I feel real bad she's caught up in this. I don't want to ruin her visit."

"She don't have to know what's going on."

"But she already asked about the bruises."

"What'd you say?"

"I told her it was none of her business. I don't know that she's old enough to understand."

"Well, she's got plenty of time to find out about this kind of sorry affair." Irene heard the door squeal open and bump shut. She took a deep breath but felt oddly deflated.

"Morning, Grandma, what's for breakfast?"

Startled, Grandma jumped a little, almost spilling the bowl of batter she was stirring. "Morning, Irene. How you feel about pancakes? Grandpa's old war buddy sent us some real Vermont maple syrup."

"I've only had Karo syrup, not real maple. Wait'll Lucy hears about this. She was reading some story where maple syrup came straight out of a tree. Is that true?"

"Sure is, honey. Seems to me you deserve something special on a vacation."

"How long will Mrs. Davis be staying?" asked Irene.

"Hard to say, Li'l Bit. Maybe she'll go tomorrow, maybe not." Grandma concentrated on her bowl of batter.

"Grandma? How'd I get my nickname?"

"From the minute we laid eyes on you, you were tiny, with black hair standing straight up on your head. Like a little paintbrush you were. Your grandpa Hutto took one look at you and said you sure looked like a little bit of spunk. Now, who would have thought a nickname like that would stick on such a young lady?" Irene wished it would unstick. Li'l Bit was so babyish for someone twelve.

Grandpa came back at noon and spent the day with Jimmy, and Irene helped out around the barn. Little kids have it easy, thought Irene. Jimmy plays as if he hasn't a worry in the world. She knew in her heart it wasn't true for Jimmy, and her eyes filled with tears. I hope Grandpa's chat will work, she wished. Why would anyone marry a man like that? Wasn't running off with someone supposed to be romantic? Lucy was always reading about those moony things and saying she was going to live in Paris and run off with a romantic Frenchman and write stories. There must be a way to find out about a person before you ran away. Irene couldn't believe that Lurleen or anybody would marry someone who pushed her around before, while they could still change their minds. Lurleen didn't look like she was capable of standing up for anything just now. I wonder if she was always like this? One thing was sure, Irene vowed silently, I'll never marry anybody like that or let any of my family do it either.

Late in the afternoon they heard a truck sputtering up their road. Lurleen froze at the sink, dropping the green beans she was cleaning.

"Hmmm," said Grandpa, walking over toward Jimmy playing near the door. "We're awfully popular lately."

"It's Papa! Mama, come quick, Papa's come to get us!" Jimmy cried.

"Settle down, Jimmy," said Lurleen. "Go put your things in the bag."

Irene thought she looked scared, the way she jumped. It was a good thing Grandpa was here.

"Lurleen, remember what we told you. Anytime,

you let us know, and we'll come get you." Grandma folded up her dishrag, placed it firmly on the counter, and squared her shoulders as she looked toward the yard.

"I sure do appreciate everything. I didn't think he'd come so soon. I'd better hurry now."

"I told him tomorrow was soon enough," said Grandpa. "Guess he . . ." Grandpa caught Irene's stare. "Guess he couldn't wait. If you're not ready to go, we can tell him I'll bring you home tomorrow."

"No, that's okay. Jimmy wants to see his pa, and it really doesn't make any difference." Lurleen hurried into the bedroom to help Jimmy as the truck pulled up to the door.

Grandpa stepped outside.

"Irene," called Grandma, "would you go in there and help Lurleen pack up?" She followed Grandpa outside as Irene said, "Yes'm."

"Can I carry the baby?" she asked Lurleen.

"If it's not too much bother, that'd be real nice. I sure appreciate your help with Jimmy," said Lurleen, looking embarrassed and fixing their packet of things.

"Mrs. Davis . . ." began Irene. "Why are you . . ."

Lurleen turned at the doorway and asked, "Excuse me?"

Irene remembered Grandma's admonition and quickly said, "Nothing, oh nothing."

Lurleen shrugged and went outside, Irene following with the baby.

"Well, there you are, Sugar. Boy, it's sure good to set eyes on you." A tall, handsome young man leaned casually against the hood of the truck, Jimmy tucked happily in his arms. "Who's this pretty young thing carrying Junie?" He gave Irene a warm smile.

"That'd be my granddaughter Irene, my daughter Mae's oldest girl." Grandpa's voice was different than she'd ever heard before; it seemed to have a warning in it.

"Howdy, Irene. You ought to have your grandpa take you over to the holding pond. Know what's been in there? An alligator. Now, that'd be a sight. Be something to tell your brothers and sisters when you go home, don't you think?"

Irene didn't know whether she was supposed to be polite or not. "Someone told us about him already, but thank you," she replied. She glanced at Grandma and tried to copy the expression on her face, not exactly friendly but not angry either. He sure didn't seem like someone mean enough to push around a woman because of a seed catalog.

"Well, we got to get going," said T.J., playfully tossing Jimmy into the truck. "Time to go, Lurleen." He glanced past Irene's grandparents and stared intently at his wife, holding out his hand.

Lurleen came around next to Irene and obediently took his hand and disappeared into the truck.

"Irene, I'll take that little charmer off your hands now," he said, holding out his arms and taking a step toward her. Irene froze.

"Why don't you just put little June on her mama's lap, honey," said Grandma. Irene was shaking, but she walked right past Mr. Davis's outstretched arms and handed the baby to Lurleen in the truck cab.

"Much obliged, Irene, Mr. and Mrs. Haskell," Lurleen called.

Her husband turned around abruptly and firmly slammed the passenger door, then got in behind the wheel and drove off.

Irene distinctly heard her grandmother say, "The

nerve of that man," as she came up and put her arm on Irene's shoulder. "Come on," she said with a sigh. "Let's go roll out some of your favorite biscuits."

Grandpa stood stock-still, watching the truck, his jaw set and a scowl on his face.

Perplexed, Irene couldn't help saying to Grandma, "He didn't seem so bad. Jimmy was real happy to see him." Irene put her arm around Grandma's familiar form and held her tight as they walked to the house.

"It's not always easy to tell about a man right off. Sweet talk doesn't always mean a kind heart. Just you remember that, Irene."

The Homeplace

"Irene, you, Ruth, and Lucy help Robert set the chairs around the yard. The boys will take down the doors and put them on the sawhorses for the tables. You gals bring out the dishes," called Grandma Haskell. It was always Grandma's undisputed position to direct the annual family dinner. "Lottie Mae, you carry this basket of silverware outside and come back in for the bread and tortillas. Homer, fill up those water pitchers and chop off the ice. When you're done with the doors, you can carry some food. And this time you'd better be careful with Aunt Belle's ham or I'll have your hide. Ruth, didn't your mama tell you to quit fussing with your hairdo and help? Mercy, Lola, doesn't your girl do anything but primp? Girls these days . . ." said Grandma, clucking her tongue.

The girls escaped with the dishes before something else occurred to Grandma.

Lola exchanged a knowing look with her two sisters. "She's just growing up, Mama," replied Lola. "I bet Irene starts soon, too."

"It'll pass," piped in Belle, coming to the aid of her big sister.

"Now, Mama, you know all girls go through it," said Mama. "We did and you survived." The sisters laughed at their mother, watching her try to wiggle out of this one.

She turned her attention to the stove, mumbling dramatically. "Don't know what this world's coming to, all this uppity back talk." She added another disapproving sound to round out her good-natured speech as she flung another piece of wood into the fire.

"Sure is a good thing Henry and I had so many kids, isn't it, Mama? I love these family reunions, even though it is a heap of work. All the children change so much in a year. Don't you think so, Belle?"

"Sure do, Mae. I can't believe little Tempest wasn't here for the last one. It seems like forever that she's been with us. I'm amazed she made it through the hurricane; thought sure I was going to lose her."

"That's how it is with young'uns, Belle, like trying

to remember being single," replied Mama. "Gets so I can't remember yesterday, let alone before Charley. Henry and I didn't even have a year married before he was born, and after Irene it seems to have taken a minute and all of a sudden there's eight of 'em under-foot. If it wasn't for Sydney, I'd think I'd dreamed most things I do remember about being young. Mama, is this your pie?" she continued, lining up the bowls of food everyone had brought.

"That's my new pecan pie recipe; the old one's over by the stove. I knew I'd never hear the last of it if I didn't bring that, too. Anything you can't remember before you married, ask me. You did some things aren't so easy to forget. I swear, Irene could be your twin half the time."

"Irene's sure grown up since that trip through the cactus," said Belle. "When I look at little Tempest I see Lucy. Looks like Tempest will have our thick hair, too."

"It's only right, Belle," said Lola, "since neither you nor Lucy would've been here without yours. I still get chills when I think about it."

"Girls, quit dawdling over past miseries and get busy putting all this food on the tables. The men are going to be coming back soon and everyone will be mighty hungry. You know everybody has their favorite and how fast the food disappears. Now, where are those gals? It can't take this long to set those chairs." Grandma walked over to the screen door, wiping her hands on a towel. "And where's that young lady Ruth? I want them to take out the slaw and tomatoes."

"Probably gawking at Ruby and her fiancé," said Mama. "They went to take a walk an hour ago and Ruth seemed to be all moony over them getting married."

"It's not every day her big sister decides to marry. Ruth is fifteen now and getting notions of her own. I swear, she drives me to distraction with all her primping and posing." Lola waved her dish towel for emphasis.

Homer slammed the door once again as he came back for some more bowls of food.

"You seen those girls, Homer?" asked Mama.

"They were talking to Ruby before, but I think Ruth is with Irene and Lucy out back," he replied.

"Homer Hardy, keep your fingers out of the peach preserves! And don't slam that door again. If you see the girls or Robert, send them back to help, you hear?"

"Yes'm, Grandma. How's Uncle Norm's coon dogs, Aunt Lola?"

"Homer, I can see when you're stalling for a bite off the platter. Now, if you were smart, you'd take all this outside like I asked and snitch a piece where we can't see you."

"Yes'm, Grandma, I'm going." He picked up the fried chicken and struggled out the door with it balanced under his nose.

"Irene, Lucy!" he called. Robert was lounging out of sight behind the big tree, eating something. "Where they off to, hey? We're doing all the work."

"Saw 'em going behind the outhouse with Ruth," replied Robert. "More food for us." Homer took the biggest piece of chicken and sat down next to him.

Behind the outhouse Irene and Lucy were awestruck. Ruth had her skirt lifted up and there underneath was a pair of shorts.

"Gosh," exclaimed Irene, "they're the best! Almost like our underwear! Where'd you get them? They're sure not in the catalog."

"Daddy says shorts are the devil's handiwork," whispered Lucy.

"My girlfriend made them, copied them out of one of those movie magazines. They're the latest thing in the picture shows. Everybody's going to be wearing them, you wait." Ruth gave Lucy and Irene a sly look. "Want to try them on?"

"I'd never . . ." began Lucy.

"Can I?" asked Irene. "How we going to do that?" They looked around.

"C'mon into the outhouse," said Ruth. "We can all fit if one of you stands on the seat." They peeked around to the front, dashed through the overgrown weeds, and quickly latched the door.

"You first," said Lucy. Irene already had her overalls half off and was squirming with anticipation. She stepped into the forbidden pants and sashayed around on top of the seat.

"How do I look? They're a mite big," she said, holding the waist. "And they sure feel funny. Wish I had a mirror."

"They don't look half bad, Irene. Why don't you step outside real quick so we can get a better look? I can't hold my breath much longer anyway," Ruth complained.

"You know you got to breathe through your mouth, Ruth. Stop being so prissy. If my daddy saw me in these, he'd tan my hide! Lucy, try 'em on." Irene turned to face the door and started to unbuckle Lucy's overalls.

"I'm not so sure, Irene. Anyway, you've got prettier legs than me." She let Irene undo the straps of her overalls, dropping them to the floor. After bending to take out her foot, she kicked the overalls toward the gap under the door. Suddenly, she straightened up and struggled to climb up next to Irene.

"Hey, what's the matter, are you—"

"Snake!" screamed Lucy, scrambling to safety. Ruth looked at her feet and jumped up next to the girls, all of them trying not to fall in the hole.

"Rattler," whispered Irene as the snake began to coil its substantial length not one foot in front of them. They looked at one another and at the same moment began to scream.

"Help! Rattler!"

"It's a diamondback!"

"Everybody shut up—it's going to strike!" They flattened themselves against the rear wall.

Suddenly the door burst open. A rattlesnake was serious business. Homer and Robert held the garden shovel and a rake ready. They took a quick look and smacked the snake's head flat to the floor, then flipped it outside. They'd killed it, like Daddy taught them. The boys looked up at the girls huddled and pale on the seat and their mouths dropped open.

"Look at your legs, Irene!" exclaimed Robert, whistling.

"Irene, you're going to catch it for sure. You know how Daddy feels about those."

"Don't you dare tell, either of you," threatened Irene.

"Foot stuck in your pants, Lucy?" asked Homer with his usual smirk.

"Hush up, you two," hissed Ruth. "Don't anyone have to know if you don't—"

Ruth was interrupted by shrieks from the anxious women as they spotted the girls. Almost immediately, Daddy, Charley, and Thomas came running up with shovels. They stopped abruptly in front of the out-house, behind the women.

"What the? . . . ." said Daddy. "Irene, where'd you get those?" He looked at Ruth. "Get out of those things this minute and come out here and explain this nonsense." He slammed the door shut and turned to face the women. Daddy looked at their faces and said to his wife, "Mae, you best remind your daughter she's not too old to get her backside switched! I told you those things bring nothing but trouble, and no daughter of mine is going to walk around like some carnival side-show." He mumbled to Charley and Thomas to come and finish their work, and stomped off toward the barn.

The girls came out and faced the women. Grandma had a dish towel over her mouth and Aunt Belle and Aunt Lola had their lips shut tight.

"Give me those short pants, Irene," said Mama. "Ruth, you're old enough to know better. Y'all finish these tables, and we'll talk about this later." They hurried back to the kitchen, holding the shorts at arm's length, their heads close together. Irene wondered why their shoulders were shaking.

"Mae," Irene could hear Grandma saying, "you see what I mean?" Irene wished she could overhear the rest; it was something about apples not falling far from the tree.

"Bet James Tilley would've liked to seen you," said Homer to Irene. She was about to answer when she remembered something more important.

"We have to see about this fiancé of Ruby's," she said.

"What d'you mean?" asked Robert.

"It's up to us to see if he's as nice as Ruby thinks," she replied. "Don't ask me so many questions. I've got my reasons. You just do like I said and come up with something so we can tell what he's like when he's not trying to impress Uncle Norm and everybody." She started off toward the house. "We've got to get the tables ready, c'mon."

Homer and Robert exchanged a look.

"Yeah, after _we_ did all the work," said Homer, following.

There were so many bowls and platters on the tables it looked like the state fair.

"No finer food in the county," commented Daddy as everyone crowded around the full tables and filled their plates. "Nothing I like better than everyone's best cooking at the same meal."

There was always cheerful confusion as all the relatives tried to put a little of everything on their plate and find a place to sit. The children gathered on the porch steps—even Ruth, who for once wanted to keep her distance from the adults. There were a couple moments of quiet while there was some serious eating. Belle's ham and Mama's fried chicken always disappeared before anything else.

"You didn't get any fried chicken, Aunt Belle. Want me to hand you a piece?" asked Charley.

"I'm never going to eat another piece of chicken or an egg as long as I live. Charley, don't you put that in front of my face. My apologies, Mae," she added, "you know it's not personal."

"How about some for you, Lucy?" Homer poked his sister and made a clucking sound.

"I warned you before, young man," said Daddy. "We're all mighty thankful we didn't fare as poorly as some others during the hurricane. And it's more of a blessing to have little Tempest born as healthy as could be just a month later."

"Say, Henry, when are you going to get one of those new tractors?" asked Uncle Norm. "They sure do make quick work of a day's plowing. I'm saving up for one myself."

"Well, Norm, it seems kind of strange to me not to have your hand in the earth. All I'd need would be a breakdown from the noisy thing in the middle of plowing. I hear they do all kinds of things, though. Going to go see Connors's new one next week. Guess you can't stop progress, even in these tough times."

"Ruby, how'd you meet your young man, here?" asked Grandpa Hutto.

"I was visiting my friend over in Kingsville and he was visiting her brother. We got to talking and before we knew it, we were getting along. And here we are." She beamed, taking her fiancé by the arm. He turned beet red and smiled shyly at her in return.

Homer leaned over to Irene and whispered, "He seems right nice to me."

"Sometimes people aren't as sweet as they talk," she whispered back. "You better figure out a way to find out what I asked you. I'm not fooling."

"I hear you've got to ride the school bus to Robstown High this fall, Irene," said Aunt Lola. "Lucky for you they're changing the dirt into caleche, or macadam, whatever they call it. Maybe it won't get stuck in the mud as many times as last year."

"Isn't caleche when they put in the crushed shells?" Mae asked.

"Yep," confirmed Grandpa Haskell.

Grandma Haskell looked at her daughter. "Mae, maybe now you'll start driving that new Ford truck, instead of those quirky mules."

At the mention of the mules Irene bent her head over her plate so no one could catch her eye. She hoped Homer wouldn't jump in.

"Going to be strange to have you with me on the school bus, Irene," said Charley. "Whaddaya think? You ready?"

"I bet James Tilley thinks it's fine and dandy," blurted Homer. "He'd hate to go anywhere without Irene."

"Then I get to ride Sydney to school," said Robert with glee.

"You can't!" cried Irene. "He won't like it! And what if you're late coming home and it's my turn? Mama, tell him he can't!"

"Irene, you know we need Sydney. The boys are

getting too big to share one horse. And since you figured out those blinders, he's as well behaved as the others. Maybe you and I can take him out together on the weekends with a picnic lunch," said Mama. She leaned back from the table and bent over toward the steps to give Irene a wink.

"We can take some of your fried chicken, right, Mama?" Irene smiled smugly at Robert.

"Sounds all right to me, honey," replied Mama. "And next week we've got to get to Robstown and find you some pretty new school shoes."

Irene thought she would burst, she felt so fine. Maybe it's not that bad being the oldest girl, she thought. "Guess I'll have another piece of corn bread," she said, getting up from the porch steps to refill her plate.

"I declare, Li'l Bit, I think you're a head taller since last summer. You're going to need a new nickname. Come to think of it, you'll always be Li'l Bit to me. I'm not shrinking down just yet." Grandpa Hutto patted his ample stomach and helped himself to some more slaw and potato salad.

After all the desserts had vanished and the dishes

were clean, everyone began to gather up their belongings. For some it was a long ride home.

"Homer, when are you going to do what I asked you?" whispered Irene. "Ruby and her fella are getting ready to leave and we have to see how he's going to treat Ruby before it's too late."

"Don't you worry, we got it figured," he replied quietly.

"You sure are all fired up about it, Irene. What put a bee in your bonnet, anyway?"

"Hush up, Robert, I told you never mind about why. You both just better have come up with something good."

Homer and Robert snickered. "It's pretty darn good, don't you fret."

Ruby and her fiancé walked over to the side table hand in hand, just like they went everywhere.

"Bet he can't even go to the outhouse without her," commented Homer.

"They're in love, he doesn't want to be parted from her." Lucy sighed.

"We'll see," said Homer.

The happy couple said their good-byes and Ruby

helpfully lifted her fiancé's hat off the side table. Her piercing screech reverberated throughout the farmhouse. He threw himself in front of Ruby protectively, wrapping his arms around her backward and fairly lifting her off her feet while backing away.

Daddy and Grandpa Haskell raced over to the side table. Grabbing the heavy dictionary off its stand, Daddy raised it in the air on his way to the table. Tail raised, its head tucked down with a mean curve, a coiled, sand-colored rattler was about to strike.

"Don't!" shouted Robert and Homer together. "It's stuffed!" They dashed under Daddy's arm and grabbed the trophy off the table, thrusting it under Ruby's face. "See?"

Ruby began screaming again. Homer was lifted off the floor by Grandpa Hutto. Daddy grabbed Robert by the collar.

"Of all the fool things! . . ." sputtered Daddy.

"Let them alone," cried Irene, "it was just a joke. We didn't know Ruby would get so scared."

"Rattlers are never a joke," fumed Daddy. "I'd've thought you'd know better, particularly today, young lady. Y'all are going to see me outside right quick."

"It's all right, Mr. Hutto," interrupted Ruby's knight in shining armor. "Might have done it myself if I'd've thought of it. Mighty fine speciman you got there. Who caught him?" He still had his arm around poor Ruby, who was beginning to get her color back and catch her breath. Grandma Haskell had brought a cold cloth and was dabbing at Ruby's face. She gave Irene a look out of the side of her eye.

Irene turned and smiled at Homer and Robert.

"Guess he'll do," she said quietly.

"Isn't he wonderful?" sighed Lucy. "Where's my diary, anybody seen it?" she asked excitedly.

"Haven't seen that fella since I had it stuffed," said Grandpa Hutto. "Matter of fact, I think it's been stored out there in the bunkhouse next to the barn. Right proud of it, I was. Did I ever tell you young'uns how I killed him?" he asked, looking around for his audience. "Notice how his head's not all squished up?"

"Don't get started now, Daddy," said Mama. "Ruby and her young man were just about to leave, as I recall. Henry, let's you and me see them safely out the door before another one of our children tries to welcome him to the family." Mama took Ruby by one arm and Daddy by the other and propelled them both toward the door.

"I think we'd better be getting on the road, too," said Joseph. They waved to the young couple and the others and took a moment to look up at the clear, starry night.

"Sure is quiet after everyone's gone, isn't it?" asked Mama. "I swear, all the children are growing up so fast. Ruby's getting married! Charley's talking about joining the army after high school. Ruth is hoping to go to beauty school. And I hear Mr. Connors's going to let them drill for oil."

"Oil? Now that could be interesting. Maybe President Roosevelt's not the only good thing going to happen to us farmers. But what I can't believe is Irene going off to high school," said Daddy.

The screen door slammed and Irene wiggled in between them under Daddy's arm.

"Ruby says they're moving to Kansas City," Irene said thoughtfully. "No matter where I go, this is always going to be my Homeplace, won't it?"

Mama smiled at Irene and nodded.

"Just as sure as you'll always be Daddy's Li'l Bit."

Afterword

For thousands of years, family history has been passed down to the next generation through oral storytelling. Today we can share stories in many different ways—through photographs, movies, books, and even on the Internet. It was by way of good old-fashioned yarn spinning—a true art form—that *Tales from the Homeplace* were collected. And now, for the first time, they are passed down in written form.

The incidents in these tales *are* true. There was a panther who lost his dinner because of Irene's ingenuity. Sydney did live to be twenty years old, never allowing anyone to pass him. The disastrous hurricane made the national newspapers, and cactus always lays in wait for careless victims. Most of us will experience our own "Hunt," and the situation in "The Visit" is all too common. Though Irene didn't actually star in all of these adventures, we hope that through her eyes you can experience life on a Texas farm during a difficult yet exciting era.

Today, Irene's younger sister Dollie Mae and her husband, Chatter, live in the remodeled Homeplace. The Texas countryside is still as flat as it was during the 1930s, and everyone is still welcomed back whenever they want to visit. Even though the family is now scattered far from the Homeplace, the bond Irene shared with her siblings remains. Perhaps you will ask your own family about their history, and perhaps, like Irene, you may discover you are more like your family than you ever imagined.

DATE			